SEND SUPERINTENDENT WEST

SEND SUPERINTENDENT WEST

John Creasey

CHARLES SCRIBNER'S SONS
NEW YORK

Library of Congress Cataloging in Publication Data

Creasey, John.
Send Superintendent West.

I. Title.
PZ3.C6153Sf3 [PR6005.R517] 823'.9'12 76-11735
ISBN 0-684-14730-0

1 3 5 7 9 11 13 15 17 19 C/C 20 18 16 14 12 10 8 6 4 2

Printed in the United States of America

F

CONTENTS

I

THE SNATCH

THE car moved swiftly, quietly, through the dark night. The driver sat back, relaxed but watchful. The man by his side sat upright, body tensed; a third man, in the back, perched on the edge of his seat and rested one arm on the back of the front seat. Behind them, the heart of London was quiet in sleep; at two in the morning only the night-birds prowled. On the periphery of the sprawling, giant city, houses built of dark-red brick stood solid on either side of tree-lined roads. Here and there a light showed at a window, dull yellow. Each house had its low brick wall, separating it from its neighbour; hedges grew thickly, giving privacy to house and garden.

The driver flicked on his head-lights.

'Put them out,' ordered the man by his side.

The driver ignored him. They neared a corner, bright light shining on the windows of a house directly in front, dazzling, warning. The driver slowed down.

'You should've turned right,' the passenger next to him said.

'I'm going to turn right.' The driver cut the corner, allowed the beams to sweep the empty road ahead, then switched into darkness. 'We can get away quicker,' he said.

'How much farther?' asked the passenger behind him.

'Two minutes. Maybe three.'

The driver's relaxed manner did not change. Driving with side-lights only, he turned twice again. A house with white walls loomed out of the darkness, tall trees black against the white. He slowed down, switched off the engine, and braked gently; the car stopped with hardly a sound. He switched off the side-lights, and all was dark.

'Ed,' he said softly, 'you get out and wait by the wall. Stay there unless you see or hear anyone around. Jay, you come with me as far as the gate. I might need some help. Ed' – he spoke in the same tone; flat, lifeless – 'keep off the bottle.'

'Sure,' muttered Ed. 'Sure.'

They got out. The driver closed the doors to the first catch to avoid slamming. Ed moved to the wall, the others walked to a corner, a few yards away. The house they were going to enter was built in a shallow cul-de-sac, off the street itself.

No lights shone anywhere.

Round the corner, the driver said: 'Stay here, Jay. Watch Ed. We'll have to do something about Ed.' From the sound of his voice, the darkness hid a smile no one would want to see. 'Stay right here.'

'Okay. But Mac —'

'Not you,' Mac said. 'Not you, as well as Ed.'

'You don't have to worry about me. But are you sure the kid won't wake up?'

'The kid won't wake up,' Mac said. 'None of them will wake up. They'll still be asleep, two hours from now, when we reach the airport. Everything's fixed.'

'That's fine.'

'You watch Ed.'

Mac gripped the other's forearm, then moved away, rubber-soled shoes making little sound. He could make out the shape of the iron gate of the house which stood squat and dark against the cloudy sky. Wind soughed down, rustling the leaves on trees and bushes. It was the middle of September, neither cold nor warm.

He reached the gate and opened it, then slowly pushed it back. He bent down and hooked it to a stumpy post in the ground, so that it couldn't swing to. He stepped on to grass and walked on this as far as the garage. Inside there was a ladder. He did not stop at the garage, but followed a gravel path leading to the rear of the house, and paused by the back door. Behind him was a square of lawn, tennis-court size, around it flower-beds, beyond the lawn a vegetable-garden hidden by ramblers proliferating about a rustic wooden fence.

It would take only a minute to force the catch, and there was a chance that the door wasn't even locked. The people here, overwhelmed with the opiate they had been given, should be asleep in their chairs; unless they had staggered up to their bedroom.

The child would have had his dinner much earlier than the parents, for the Shawns had strict ideas about bringing up children.

Mac had telephoned the house at midnight and again at one o'clock, and there had been no answer; evidence that everything had gone according to plan. The lock of the back door clicked, and he withdrew a pick-lock, slipping it into his pocket before turning the handle and pushing. The door yielded. He stepped inside, closing it behind him, and put on a flashlight. The beam stabbed at a stainless steel sink and big metal taps, then moved until it shone beyond the shiny white tiled wall and through the open door. He knew the house well, and found his way easily through the three ground-floor rooms. In the dining-room, he grinned as the white light shone on the littered table, on some half-eaten ham, limp salad in a bowl, a percolator, dirty cups, plates and knives. They hadn't been able to finish the meal, they'd been so tired.

Mac went to the table.

He was short, with very broad shoulders, stocky but quick in his movements. His glossy dark hair was brushed straight back from his forehead, he had small features in a big face, a tawny skin, and unexpectedly clear grey eyes. If one failed to notice the thin lips his appearance, on first sight, was likeable.

He picked up the cups and saucers and took them to the kitchen, putting them on the metal draining-board, then went back for the percolator, which was nearly full. Resting the flashlight on the window-ledge, he washed the cups and saucers, emptied the milk jug and washed this also. He opened the refrigerator, took out a quart bottle of milk, half full, and emptied it. He washed this bottle, too. Next he took a pint bottle of milk out of his pocket, poured it into the empty quart bottle, then poured some from that into the jug.

He poured a little milk and some cold coffee into each cup, swilled it round and spilled a little into each saucer, then put the empty pint bottle back into his pocket. He ran some water to rinse the sink and remove all traces of the opiate which had been in the quart bottle of milk. He put the pure milk into the refrigerator, then carried cups and saucers, jug and percolator back into the dining-room, replacing them where he had found them.

His hands were cold from the water, except at the finger tips, which were protected by sticking-plaster. He rubbed them together as he went upstairs. The door of the main bed-room was ajar, and the Shawns lay together on the big double bed, Shawn nearer the door, his dark head close to his wife's, which was almost platinum blonde. She lay on her back, Shawn on his left side, facing her, one hand limp on her breast. She wore a filmy pink nightdress or pyjamas, but Shawn hadn't undressed completely. Mac went across to the bed, buried his fingers in Shawn's hair, and tugged. Shawn's head jerked back, but he didn't make a sound or flicker an eyelid. Mac shone his torch into the woman's face and stood there for a long time. He had a reputation that was bad even among people who rejected the ordinary moral codes; his expression showed why. It was hungry; it was brutal.

'Boy,' he said, 'it would only take five minutes. What's to stop me?'

He moved towards her, hand outstretched, but suddenly drew back, turned on his heel, and went out, leaving the door still ajar. Across the wide landing, another door was open. Inside, a boy of about ten years lay on his side in a single bed, his black hair making him look like a miniature edition of his father. The bedclothes were pulled out of the side of the mattress, and only blue-and-white striped pyjamas covered the boy.

Mac bent over him, seeing features which were startlingly like Belle Shawn's; then, turning from the bed, he took a small suitcase from the bottom of the wardrobe. In this he packed the clothes the boy had taken off, now folded on a chair, toothbrush, paste, clean handkerchiefs, shirts, socks and a spare suit. Then he went back to the bed, carrying a top coat, sat the boy up, and forced his arms into the sleeves. None of this took very long. He hoisted the boy up to his left shoulder, managing to retain the flashlight in his left hand, picked up the suitcase and went out of the bedroom and downstairs.

He had to put the case down to open the back door, hold the door steady with his foot, pick up the case, and then back out. A gust of wind caught him by surprise, pulling the door free and slamming it. The noise shattered the quietness, making Mac hiss.

The wind ruffled the boy's hair.

Mac kept to the grass, and watched the windows of the neighbouring houses. No lights came on. When he reached the gate, Jay was moving towards him.

'You okay?'

'Yeah. Get going.' Mac held out the case, and Jay took it. He was taller than Mac, and thinner, with a small head and wide brimmed hat; the two men made a sharp contrast.

Ed was at the corner, burly, podgy, scared.

'You hear that door bang?'

'I banged it,' Mac said. 'Take the kid.'

'If anyone wakes up . . .'

'Just take the kid.'

Ed gulped and obeyed, cradling the boy in his arms. Then he bent down, as Jay opened the rear door of the car, and lifted the boy inside, sat him on the seat and pushed him towards the far corner. By the time he had finished, Mac was at the wheel and Jay was beside him, case on his knees. Ed closed the door, which didn't fasten properly.

'Leave it,' Mac ordered.

Ed kept a hand on the handle to stop the rattling. Mac didn't start the engine, but took off the hand-brake; the gradient was steep enough to start the car rolling, and they moved a hundred yards or so before he switched on the engine and the side-lights. The engine made little noise. Near a corner, Mac put on the head-lights and this time Ed didn't protest. The lights swept the road ahead as they turned the corner, and out of the night came a man.

He was at a gate. He was dressed in dark clothes that looked black, and a helmet. A flashlight seemed to be fastened somewhere on to his stomach. He didn't move, yet seemed to leap in front of their eyes. They could see his big face and heavy moustache. He was there only for a moment before they passed him. Mac kept the head-lights on.

Ed turned his head and stared out of the back window. As they turned a corner, he moved round slowly, moistening his lips.

'You see him?'

'We're not blind,' Jay said.

'A cop.'

'We don't have to worry about English cops,' Jay said. He sounded as if he were trying to convince himself.

'We don't have to worry about anything,' Mac stated flatly.

'Even in this goddamned country it isn't a crime to drive by night, although maybe you'd think it was, they go to bed so early. Ed' – he maintained the steady monotone – 'you've got work to do. It should be easy, you have kids of your own. Open that case – give him the case, Jay – and get the kid dressed. We still have an hour. Take it easy. Don't forget his underpants.' Mac sounded as if that was meant for a joke. 'You want to close the door?'

Ed took another glance out of the back window, slammed the door, then began to dress the kidnapped child.

2

ASSIGNMENT

ROGER West lay in bed, eyes closed, breathing heavily, giving a fair imitation of a snore. He heard the door open, and stealthy movements inside the room. He didn't open his eyes. Rustling sounds followed, and he knew he wouldn't need to keep up the pretence much longer. Cups chinked as a tray was put on the small table next to the bed on his side, and he opened his eyes and looked through his lashes at the broad face of Martin-called-Scoopy, his elder son, beaming down at him.

''Morning, Pop!'

'I'll pop you,' Roger said, gruffly. He struggled up to a sitting position as Richard, his younger son, half a head taller than Martin, entered the bedroom. Both boys had the glow of health in cheeks and eyes, and in that moment something in their expressions made them remarkably alike, although usually they were so different.

'Your mother's all right or you wouldn't be looking so pleased with yourselves. You want something, or you wouldn't both be here. No.'

He began to pour out tea.

At twenty-one, Martin was more than old enough to know his own mind, and he was studying art at the Chelsea College of Painting, working in the evenings and weekends. Richard was working at a film studio near London, hoping to write scripts for a living. It was seldom that either came to him for anything, these days; for them both to come at once was rare indeed.

'If it's no,' Richard said, 'you're in for a shock, Dad.'

Roger sipped his tea.

'Well, one of us is,' he temporized. There was something in their minds he couldn't guess. It wasn't April Fool's Day. It wasn't his birthday. It wasn't —

Suddenly, he remembered; it was the first day of the Summer Sales, and Janet had said she wanted to go to Oxford Street. She was desperate for a new Autumn outfit; he must have slept on – but no, it wasn't too late – just before eight.

'All right,' he said. 'Shock me.'

'Mum forgot to get any money out of the bank,' Richard said, 'and you've only a pound in your wallet. So she's gone to get a place in the queue at Debb's, and somehow you have to take her some money.'

'Twenty-four years wed, she complained,' said Scoop, 'and she still doesn't know where you keep your secret hoard. She turned the place upside down.'

'I still keep it at the bank, and she knows it,' Roger said. 'I'll have to change a cheque at a shop on the way.'

It was an empty kind of morning, without Janet; emptier as soon as the boys had left. Boys? And Richard a bare year younger than Martin? He laughed the thought away as he went downstairs to get his own breakfast; but there was instant porridge, bacon and eggs in the frying pan, everything ready for him.

He caught Janet a few yards from the main entrance at

Debb's, one of several hundred women; and once he had put thirty pounds into her hands there was a surge forward as the door opened.

'See you!' Roger called.

'Thank you, darling,' she said breathlessly, and was carried with the crowd, dark-haired, neat in a plain grey suit, young for her forty-odd years, and at that moment, not thinking of him at all.

Roger got back into the car, restarted the engine, and was soon caught up in the stream of early morning traffic. There had been a time when he had arrived at Scotland Yard morning after morning with a sense of excitement and expectation, but now he knew what to expect. Crime had a thousand variations, and he seemed to know them all. For a Detective Superintendent, murder cases had lost their stimulating effect. The paperwork and routine of a senior Criminal Investigation Department officer kept him at the desk more and more, and there were times when the pleasant office was like a jail; or like a cell at the squat grey building of Cannon Row Police Station, which looked as if it were in a corner of the Yard premises, but in fact was not. All the small windows were barred. Big Ben could look down on its slate roof from the tower of the Houses of Parliament, but couldn't make the drab grey look bright even on this fine warm summer morning.

Roger parked his car and walked up the steps. Good morning, good morning, 'morning, 'lo, Handsome; such greetings had become a ritual. Calling him 'Handsome' West had, too. So had sitting at his desk and looking through mail and reports. But today it depressed him. Glancing through the dossier of an old lag, due at Great Marlborough Street Court on a charge for the thirteenth time, Roger knew exactly what he would say, what the magistrate would say and what he would look like, peering over his spectacles; what lies the accused would utter, forlornly, what the magistrate's clerk would intone, and what everything and everybody would be like. He lit a cigarette, yawned, scribbled a few pencilled notes, and the telephone bell rang.

'West speaking.'

'Good morning, sir.' It was a girl. 'The American Embassy – I'm sorry, the United States Embassy – is on the line. They wanted the Assistant Commissioner or the Commander, but they're not in, sir.'

'I'll speak to the Embassy,' Roger said. At least this was different.

'Just a moment, please,' the girl said.

Almost at once a man with a clipped North American accent said: 'Is that Superintendent West?'

'Yes, sir. Good morning.'

'Good morning. Mr West, we need your help here, and we need it very badly and very fast. I am Tony Marino, and I'll wait in my office until you arrive. You'll find an impatient and worried man, Mr West.'

Roger could have asked questions, and could have been formal. Instead, he said simply:

'I'll be with you in fifteen minutes, Mr Marino.'

'I'm very grateful.' The American's voice died in the click of the telephone.

Roger stood up, took his trilby from a wall-peg and hurried to the door. If he saw the Commander, CID or Hardy, the new Assistant Commissioner, he would have to report this, and he didn't want to miss it. He saw no one of superior rank, but as he reached the ground floor in the lift, Chief Inspector Bill Sloan, big, fresh-faced, boyish-looking, was waiting to step in.

'Just the man,' said Roger. 'I've had a call from the American Embassy, they want someone in a hurry. It fell in my lap, and I'm keeping it. Tell the Commander or the AC.'

Sloan grinned. 'I'll forget it long enough for you to get there.'

It took eighteen minutes to reach Grosvenor Square. In the bright morning sunshine, a dozen American tourists were busy with their cameras near the Roosevelt statue, big American cars, dwarfing the English ones, were parked nearby. He expected some formality, not the youthful-looking man waiting just inside the hall of the big new Embassy building which some people hated, and some thought was magnificent, who said:

'Superintendent West, isn't it?'

'Yes.' Roger looked his surprise.

'I saw you in court one day, sir. I wasn't the prisoner!'

Roger smiled, liking the clean-cut look of his guide. They went in a lift to the third floor, and walked along two passages before the man tapped on a wooden door which had no name on the outside. A voice said 'come in', but it wasn't Marino's; this was a small office, with another door leading off, standing ajar.

'Superintendent West,' said Roger's guide.

'You certainly haven't lost much time, sir.' The secretary, who might have been his guide's twin brother, took over. 'We'll go right in.'

The room beyond was large, carpeted, warmer than Roger liked. There were some portraits on the wall, including one in oils of George Washington, and a coloured photograph of Lyndon Johnson. Sitting directly beneath this was a heavily built man who seemed huge, his shoulders broad and powerful-looking, in a pale grey, light-weight jacket. He had a wide face and big but pleasant features, with dark hair cut short and standing upright; there was no pomade on it, and it gave him a kind of unfinished look. His square chin was clean-shaven, and he was obviously a man who needed to shave twice a day. His eyes were velvety brown in colour, and very clear. He smiled and put out a hand, but didn't get up.

'Good of you to come in such a hurry, Superintendent. All right, Herb, I'll ring if I want you.' Herb, the secretary, was pushing a chair up for Roger, and went out as Roger sat down. Marino slid a lacquered box of cigarettes across the desk. 'American or English,' he said.

Roger felt that he was being photographed by those brown eyes; felt, too, as if he were being weighed on a mental balance. In a sudden flash, he realized how so many minor criminals felt when he sat weighing them up. He chose an English cigarette, and Marino flicked a lighter.

'Thanks. How can I help?'

'Well,' said Marino, 'you could help several ways, I guess, but the best way would be to go out and find the boy. I've good reason to think that the ten-year-old son of David Shawn, who is on a special mission in the United Kingdom, was kidnapped last night, from a house on the Chiswick and Ealing borders. I don't know why it happened, but we want the boy back because of what it means to his parents, and we also want him back because of what this might do to David Shawn, whose work is high on the Secrets List.'

Roger pondered, and asked: 'Who knows about the kidnapping?'

'You and I, Lissa Meredith, who was acting as Shawn's secretary, and Herb. In half an hour the Ambassador will also know. Lissa discovered what had happened. She had a key to the house, and was due at work at eight o'clock, but she arrived ten minutes late. She found everyone asleep, and couldn't wake David or Belle Shawn, his wife. The child's bed was empty, his clothes and a suitcase had been taken away. Lissa closed up the house, went to see the day maid, and told her not to go in. Then she telephoned me. I sent a man out to watch the house so that she could come here.'

'Why didn't she send for a doctor?' Roger asked.

'She's had some nursing experience, and decided the Shawns weren't in danger.' Marino smiled; he had fine, very white teeth. 'I'd like you to go to the house and see what you can make of the situation, Mr West. Can you do that without consulting anyone else?'

'I can but it would be wiser to have a word with the Commander or the Assistant Commissioner.'

Marino picked up a telephone, told Herb to get one or the other on the line, then put the instrument back.

'I know Ricky Shawn,' he said. 'I would hate to have anything really bad happen to him. Have you any family?'

'Two boys,' Roger said.

Marino nodded, and they waited in silence while Roger tried to pierce the shroud of mystery which Marino had deliberately created. There were always difficulties about an investigation which had to be kept secret, especially in a kidnapping case.

'Are the Shawns wealthy?' he asked suddenly.

'Very.'

'Why a suburban house and just a daily maid?'

'They've only been there since Ricky arrived, and I imagine Belle Shawn is having fun playing at housework. Lissa doesn't think she will for long.'

Lissa, Roger pondered; how soon would he learn more about Lissa?

The telephone bell rang, one of three on the desk.

'The middle one,' Marino said.

'The Assistant Commissioner is on the line,' said a girl, and after a moment a man with a rather hard voice asked:

'Is that you, West? What are you doing there?'

'They want us to look into a job which was pulled during the night,' Roger said. 'They're in a hurry, but they don't want to talk over the telephone.'

'All right, see what you can make of it,' Hardy said. 'Don't let them high-pressure you, though.'

Roger pushed the telephone away, and asked:

'Who will take me to the house?'

'Lissa Meredith will,' Marino answered. He lifted the telephone, and went on: 'Ask Lissa to come right away,

Herb.' Replacing the receiver, he continued: 'You'll get along with Lissa, but then I guess you get along with most people.'

'I try to,' Roger said. 'As this is hush-hush to begin with, why not start the right way? I won't leave the Embassy with Miss Meredith —'

'Mrs Meredith.'

'Oh! I'll have a word with her here, and pick her up somewhere on the way – on the Bayswater Road just beyond the park gates, say. I may be recognized, and if I'm seen leaving with David Shawn's secretary, a lot of people will put two and two together.' He waited.

'We are certainly going to get along,' Marino said, and looked up as the door opened and Lissa Meredith came in.

3

LISSA

LISSA Meredith had beautiful red hair and a smile of the kind that, a few hundred years ago, would have set armies marching and empires tumbling. It wasn't so much that she was a beauty, but that she seemed aflame with vitality. It glowed in the rich tints of her hair and the light in her honey-brown eyes and the rippling quicksilver of her movements. She wore a plain greeny-grey linen suit, with dark green piping, and a white blouse with a bow of the same piping at the neck.

'Hi, Tony,' she said, and smiled at Roger.

He had to remind himself that a child had been kidnapped and the case needed all his attention.

'Hi. Lissa, this is Superintendent Roger West of Scotland Yard. He's going out with you to Shawn's place. You're to wait for him at the Hyde Park Gate in Bayswater Road. Do you know it?'

'Who doesn't?' she asked. 'How soon?'

'As soon as you can get there.'

'Not quite so soon as that,' Roger said. 'I'd like to know more about the affair before we leave. The address of the house, what you found there, everything that isn't on the Secret List.'

'I could tell you on the way,' Lissa said.

'You can fill in the details on the way.'

Lissa glanced at Marino, obviously for approval, and he waved her to a chair. She didn't take it, but leaned against his desk, ankles crossed, nylon-sheathed legs slim, exciting.

'I want to find Ricky as soon as we can,' she said. 'I want to find him before Belle comes round, because any danger to him will drive her mad. She's crazy about that boy. So is David, but David's tougher. A broken Belle might break David, and we can't risk that. You just have to find the child, Superintendent.' Her voice had the warmth of fire. Roger wasn't particularly familiar with American accents, but he placed this as faintly Southern. 'The house is thirty-one Wavertree Road, Ealing, one of a thousand houses that all look the same. I left there last evening at twenty after five, and everything was normal. Ricky walked to the end of the street with me. I arrived there this morning at ten minutes after eight, and the first thing that seemed wrong was the silence. Belle often sleeps late but David is usually up early, and so is Ricky. I went upstairs, and found David and Belle so deep asleep that they wouldn't wake up.'

Roger said: 'Asleep?'

'Breathing,' she corrected. 'Under drugs, you can be sure of that. I couldn't get across to Ricky's room quickly enough. His bed had been slept in, but it was empty. His clothes were gone, and so was a suitcase – one I unpacked for him when he arrived, three weeks ago. Belle just couldn't live without him.'

Roger sensed criticism of Belle Shawn. Disapproval or

just impatience? he wondered.

'Toothbrush and things gone?' he asked.

'Yes.' Lissa stood upright. 'That was a relief, they wouldn't take his toothbrush if they didn't mean to look after him.' She probably meant 'If they meant to kill him.'

'I suppose not,' Roger said.

She said sharply: 'Don't you agree?'

'Supposing we don't take anything for granted? They would take his toothbrush if they wanted us to think that they were going to take good care of him, wouldn't they?'

She stared down at him; and now her honey-coloured eyes weren't smiling, they were nearly threatening.

'If you say that to Belle or to David,' she said, 'I won't forgive you.'

She was a new experience for Roger; working with her would be as invigorating as a walk in the teeth of a high wind.

'Did you look round the rest of the house?' he asked.

'Surely. The back door was open.'

She had been thorough, she had a mind for detail, and she had kept her head. Added to everything he had seen about her was an underlying factor which might be a truer indication of her nature; coolness in emergency.

Marino put an elbow on the polished desk, and said with a hint of impatience:

'Lissa knows the Shawns better than anyone in England. She can tell you about them on the way.'

'All right, I'm nearly ready to go,' Roger said. 'You'll have to send a doctor, quickly. The Shawns may need one. Shall I fix it with Division, or —'

'I'll fix the doctor.'

'And I'd like to call the Yard again.'

Marino gave instructions to Herb, and the others watched him as he picked up the telephone, were intent on every word he said.

He spoke to Bill Sloan, who already knew a little, and

would be as discreet as anyone.

'Bill, contact the Ealing Station,' he said. 'Have them find out who was patrolling Wavertree Road last night, the late day-duty man and the night-duty man. I want to see both officers at the Divisional station at' – he glanced at a small clock on the desk; it was a little after ten o'clock – 'noon on the dot.'

'I'll see to it,' promised Sloan.

'Thanks.' Roger put down the receiver and stood up. 'You go ahead, Mrs Meredith, in a taxi. I'll pick you up at the gate two or three minutes later. Is that all right?'

'Surely.'

Her eyes glowed approval before she turned away, waved from the door, and went out. Roger supposed that he would get used to her; that if he tried hard enough, he could become proof against her disturbing vitality.

Marino was smiling as if guessing that his thoughts were on the woman at least as much as on the case.

'One other thing, Mr West. Before you report to your superiors, you will come and see me, won't you?'

'Yes.'

'Thank you.'

Once again Marino didn't get up, simply put out a hand.

Going towards the lift, with Herb as guide, Roger realized how little Marino had said and how much he had implied; and he warned himself that he must not worry about the reasons for secrecy, this was a single problem, the finding of a kidnapped child. But the emotional factor couldn't be disregarded for long; if the boy was not back by the time his mother came round, there would probably be a lot of complications.

Lissa Meredith was standing near the gate, beautiful against the heavy summer foliage of the trees and the grass still brilliant green from summer rain. She was beside the car before he could get out, slid into the seat next to him and closed the door.

'You were on time,' she said. 'What do you want to know?'

'Everything you saw, all the details you can remember, and everything you think I ought to know about the Shawns,' Roger answered. He offered her his cigarette case. 'Down to the most minute detail.'

'Such as toothbrushes,' she said. 'I'd rather smoke my own.' She took a red packet of Pall Malls from her handbag, and flicked a lighter as Roger slid the car into the stream of traffic. 'They had gone to bed in a hurry, that's for sure. Belle's clothes were just dropped on the floor, some of David's were in a pile by the side of the bed. I don't believe that means what you probably think it means. Belle is a tidy creature by habit. Fastidious.' Again the implication of criticism, of 'too fastidious'. 'They hadn't cleared away after dinner, which was most unusual. Belle is having fun being a real housewife. Sometimes she will just put the dirty things in the washing-up machine, but she won't leave the dining-room untidy. They must have been desperately tired. Do you want me to guess?'

'Just facts, please.'

'I might guess better than you.'

'We'll guess together when we have to,' Roger said. 'Don't let's start arguing.'

She looked intently at his profile, which was very good. If there was anything wrong, it was with his chin, which was rather heavy and thrusting. He had a shortish nose and finely chiselled lips, his hat was pushed to the back of his head, showing wavy, corn-coloured hair, the colour of which almost disguised the grey. He knew that she was studying him closely.

'Who wants to argue?' There was laughter as well as submission in the words. 'The back door wasn't locked, but the front door was. None of the catches had been fastened at the windows. Belle is a nervous woman, the windows were always fastened and doors bolted.'

'Why was – why *is* she nervous?'

'I don't know of any reasons, except —' Lissa paused. 'Except that being nervous is a kind of obsession with her.'

'You don't sound as if you approve of Belle Shawn,' Roger said drily, and when that won no response, he went on: 'What do you think gives her this obsession?'

'No one's ever put her across his knee, face downwards,' said Lissa, very deliberately. 'You really want to know about her?'

'I have to know,' Roger said. 'I have to be able to judge how much notice to pay to what she says. Do you mean she is spoiled?'

'Fussed, pampered, protected against the evil world, indulged since she was able to walk. And in spite of all that,' Lissa Meredith went on, 'the better Belle often shows through, the good and adorable Belle. You're right to want to know about Belle before you talk to her.'

'You imply that she's neurotic and hard to live with?' Roger asked.

'Part of the time, that's true.'

'Is she happy?'

'Can a bundle of nerves be happy?'

'Part of the time.'

'Oh, she is. Little parts. David's been away from her a great deal. First the Korean war, then some special assignments. That is why they came to England. David's likely to be here for twelve months, perhaps longer. Then she found she couldn't bear to be without Ricky, and they sent for him. Did you really mean to ask if she's happy with David?'

'I'd like to know.'

'I can tell you he's in love with her – passionately. But it's one thing for a man to come back to a beautiful wife, to know she's waiting, another to be the patient, faithful wife. Oh, I don't think there is anything *wrong*.' He knew that she was glancing at him, and that her eyes were laughing. 'But they don't really know each other very well. Are you looking for a motive?'

'Just for facts.' He turned into a main road near Hammersmith Broadway, where five roads met and the lumbering red giants of the buses loomed over the black Humber Hawk.

'Shawn's inclined to give her her head, is he? He's too easy with her?'

'Isn't that a guess?' taunted Lissa.

'A deduction. His wife usually sleeps late, the maid arrives at nine, and Shawn and his son get up early, so someone gets the breakfast.'

Lissa laughed.

'They don't have a cooked breakfast. But you're right, David takes the easy way with Belle.'

'Has there ever been any threat to the boy?'

'I've not heard of one.'

'Do you know of anybody with a personal motive for wanting to hurt either of them?'

'No.'

'Mr Marino said they were rich,' Roger remarked after a pause.

'They were both rich at one time, but Belle lost her money. David has plenty for the two of them, but —' Lissa hesitated, as if seeking the right words, then went on very slowly. 'I think if she still had her own money, she would take Ricky and leave David high and dry. It makes it sound as if I don't like Belle, and that's not so, Superintendent. But I do think David's money holds Belle where nothing and no one else could.'

At Ealing Broadway, near the Common, where women and young children and here and there a nursemaid were sitting about or playing beneath the shade of trees, Lissa told him where to turn off for Wavertree Road. Soon they were driving along the narrow, tree-lined avenues of the housing estate. They passed countless houses which looked very much alike, the red bricked walls, the concealing hedges. Everything had the neat and tidy look that was so typically English.

From the end of Wavertree Road, Lissa directed him to the cul-de-sac, shaped like a horseshoe and with three houses in it, the Shawns' the middle of the three. This house was brick-built, the top was timbered, and the tiles were weathered to a dark red. Window frames and doors had been recently painted, and the garden was spick and span, dahlias nodding multi-coloured heads and ragged petals in the quiet wind. In the garden of the house on the right, a grey-haired woman stood looking up at Number Thirty-one.

As Roger switched off the engine, they heard a scream, then a man's voice, followed by more screaming which shattered the suburban quiet; even here the note of hysteria was clearly discernible, with its message of anguish.

Lissa Meredith was out of the car before Roger. She ran to the gate, which stood open, and flew along the yellow gravel path to the front door. The grey-haired woman stared apprehensively at her and at Roger. By the time Roger reached the porch Lissa had opened the front door and disappeared. The screaming became louder, the distorted voice made words sound like raw wounds.

'It's your fault, it's your fault, I hate you! I *hate* you, I could kill you! Get out of my way, get out, get out!'

Roger went into the hall, closed the door, saw Lissa half-way up the stairs and two people – obviously the Shawns – at the head, on the landing. Belle was struggling wildly in her husband's grasp.

4

HYSTERIA

BELLE SHAWN wore a dressing-gown, wide open; beneath it, a pair of filmy pink pyjamas. Her hair was blown about as if caught by a high wind; she was kicking at Shawn and trying to wrench her arms free. As Lissa neared them, she got one hand away, and her fingers clawed at her husband's face. Pain made him relax his grip, and Belle pulled herself free, turned and rushed down the stairs – and saw Lissa for the first time.

She screamed: 'Ricky's gone, Ricky's gone! Fetch the police, *he* won't. Fetch the police!'

She almost fell down the next few stairs, and when she was a step above Lissa, Roger could see the distortion of her face; the wild expression, the lips stretched so tautly across the large white teeth that it was like looking at a hideous mask.

Shawn was in a sleeveless vest and trousers. His face was a mask, too, but it wasn't hideous; except for the burning eyes and the barely noticeable working of the jaw it would have been expressionless. Blood welled up from two parallel scratches across his right cheek.

'Fetch the police!' screamed Belle. 'If you won't —' She caught her breath, but it was only a fleeting pause, there was no chance for Lissa to speak before she cried: 'You're as bad as he is! You're worse, get out of my way!'

Roger saw her hand rise, saw Lissa stagger to one side.

Shawn called: 'Belle!'

Belle pushed past Lissa, stumbled again, saved herself by grabbing the banister rail, then raced down the remaining stairs dressing-gown flying behind her, bare legs long and shapely, pyjama coat rucking up. She didn't see Roger until she was past Lissa. She didn't stop, but veered to the right. Guessing he would try to stop her, she put out both hands to fend him off. She was sobbing, her lips were drawn back over those large teeth, which now seemed ugly. Her eyes held the glare of madness.

Roger ducked, dived, caught her round the knees and brought her down. She struck her head heavily on the carpet, didn't cry out, but lay still. He straightened up, pulled the dressing-gown over her legs, and then knelt beside her.

The quiet was unreal, a false calm in a storm; everything about this episode seemed unreal, even the quiet note in Shawn's voice as he said:

'I'll take her.'

Roger drew back, and Shawn gathered his dazed wife in his arms and carried her upstairs. Lissa followed him without a word, and they disappeared into a room on the right. Now there was the feeling of a lull before an even greater storm. Roger had a vivid mental picture of the man, very big and powerful and with startling good looks; and of his burning eyes.

Another man appeared from the kitchen, a third to 'Herb' and his guide at the Embassy, sleek, youthful, fair, fresh-faced; his smile probably hid embarrassment.

'You take risks, Superintendent, don't you?'

'Sometimes. Who are you?'

'Mr Antonio Marino sent me, to stay around until Lissa arrived with Superintendent West from Scotland Yard. How would you like to prove you're West?'

Roger took out his wallet and flashed his CID card, gave the man time to look at it, put it away, and asked:

'How long has this screaming been going on?'

'It just blew up. Anything you would like me to do?'

'Make sure you haven't touched anything in the kitchen.'

'Only a chair.'

Roger said: 'I'll see you in a minute,' and went to the dining-room, where a telephone stood on a table near the window. He covered the receiver with his handkerchief, then dialled the Embassy. All the time footsteps thudded on the ceiling, but there was no other sound; no crying. Marino was soon on the line.

'Roger West,' announced Roger. 'That doctor isn't here, and he's needed in a hurry.'

'He'll be there very soon,' Marino promised in his lazy voice. 'I'm glad you called, Superintendent. The Ambassador and the Commissioner are to have lunch together, and the Commissioner has been good enough to agree that you come and talk to me afterwards, instead of going straight to Scotland Yard.' Roger didn't comment. 'What can you tell me?' Marino went on.

'That you will have to have some publicity, even if you say there's been a burglary,' Roger said. 'One of the neighbours probably knows what's happened – Mrs Shawn's voice can be heard a long way off. Make sure that doctor hurries, won't you?'

'He's already hurrying.' Marino sounded worried. 'Is Pete Kennedy there?'

'If he's the fair-haired man, yes. Just a moment.'

The man was Peter Kennedy. He spoke to Marino, then put the instrument down and said: 'I have to be on my way, Mr West, unless there's anything you need that no one else can give you.'

'Just evidence that you *are* Peter Kennedy.'

The other grinned, showed a badge, and gave a mock salute.

After he had gone, Roger looked about the room, inspected the cups and saucers and everything on the table, reading the story they told; that the Shawns had been overwhelmed with tiredness at the end of the meal, had dragged themselves up to bed and had 'slept' for twelve hours and more. At eight-ten when Lissa Meredith had arrived, they had been unconscious; probably they had come round half an hour or so ago.

He walked about the room, which wasn't large – perhaps fifteen feet by twenty or so. It had a fitted carpet in pearl grey, the furniture was contemporary, spindly and expensive, as far removed from utility as a mink fur coat from a coney. Everything was pleasing to the eye. There were no pictures, not even the half-expected abstracts, only three framed photographs on the mantelpiece. Roger looked at the middle picture, which was of the boy.

He had a small, sensitive, frightened face. Frightened, Roger wondered. Why did he get that impression? It was the face of a child who lacked confidence; yet it was impossible to say why Roger was so sure of this, unless he had been influenced by Lissa's strictures on the mother. The expression was one he had never seen on Martin-called-Scoopy's face, or Richard's. He had seen it on the faces of boys who had been in trouble; urchins from the street, puffed up with a braggadocio which usually collapsed when they reached the threshold of the Juvenile Court. He had seen it on the face of a neighbour's son, and learned afterwards that the couple had quarrelled day in, day out; divorce had brought the child a kind of peace.

Sensitive, then, and frightened – or lost? Yet the son of wealthy parents, with everything life could offer.

The boy was certainly like his mother in looks, and although Roger had only seen her face ravaged with grief, he realized she was a beauty; according to Lissa, a petulant beauty.

Roger examined the back door more closely, found one or two scratches, gave it more attention, and felt sure that the man or men had entered this way. In half an hour he found nothing else. He poured the dregs from each coffee-cup into small medicine bottles he found in a cupboard, after rinsing them out; he poured the milk from the jug into another bottle, placed samples of the sugar, coffee and all the food he could find into a small basket he discovered in the kitchen. All this, without destroying prints that might be there. He felt curiously on his own, and badly wanted a team; he would have settled for Bill Sloan.

He heard a movement outside the kitchen, but didn't look round. He could see the door in a small mirror hanging between the two windows. It was Lissa. She came in quietly; he didn't think stealthily. She wasn't smiling or frowning, but looked intent. He waited until she was halfway across the room, and then turned.

'Hallo.'

'Hi,' she said. 'Mr West, you've got to make David believe you'll find Ricky.'

'Have I?' Roger said heavily.

'It matters more than almost anything else you can think of. You must make him believe that you will find the boy. Even if it means faked evidence.' Her eyes demanded that of him, and he knew that she felt this need desperately. 'Because if you don't —'

'He will listen to ransom talk,' Roger suggested.

'*Ran*som,' she said. 'Yes, he will.'

She drew nearer, a hand touched his, the honey-coloured eyes had a faraway look. In a tauter voice, she said: 'You're very hard. I can tell that. But you must convince David that he will do harm, not good, by talking terms with anyone. It could be for money. It's more likely to be someone who wants to high pressure David for his secret knowledge.'

The telephone bell rang.

She turned, swift as light, towards the door, but Roger reached it just behind her and gripped her arm. She didn't try to pull herself free, just walked along the passage, speaking in a whisper.

'David will answer it upstairs. We can listen-in in

the dining-room.'

They were at the dining-room door, and she meant to reach the extension telephone first. Roger slipped past her, actually pushing her to one side as he picked up the receiver. A yard away, she stood defiant and resentful. He couldn't mistake the curiously gruff quality of Shawn's voice, although Shawn was only giving the number of the house.

A man said: 'That David Shawn?'

'Yes,' said Shawn.

'David Shawn,' repeated the caller, as if he were rolling the words round his tongue. He was English, or his voice was English, and Roger had expected an American. 'How long have you been awake?'

Shawn said: 'Long enough.'

'So you know.'

'I know,' Shawn said.

He didn't alter his tone, but Roger could picture his face, the burning eyes, the way his jaw clamped and the way his lips moved as if uttering each word caused pain.

'Don't do anything,' the caller ordered. 'Just wait until you're told what to do. Just wait.'

He rang off.

Roger held the receiver close to his ear, and could hear Shawn's heavy breathing. Slowly, that receiver went down. Lissa moved away from Roger, and swift brightness of a smile drove away the frost of her resentment.

'Was the conversation worth hearing?'

'He had orders to wait and do nothing.' Roger replaced his receiver. 'And you think he'll obey.'

'I'm afraid he will obey. I think —' Lissa paused, frowned in concentration, and then went on more rapidly, drawing closer in a conspiratorial way. 'I guessed a lot, but David told me the truth just now. He and Belle were in danger of breaking up, and only Ricky kept them together. He agreed to have Ricky here in a desperate effort to stave off the collapse. It would be a disaster to him, or he thinks it would. She will blame him, of course. She will say if he had given up his assignment and gone back home, this would never have happened to their son.'

'*Would* it have happened?'

'Shawn is important, very important, doing work only he can do. This could prey on his mind so much that he would be unable to carry on with it.'

'Sooner or later you're going to have to talk freely to me or someone at the Yard,' Roger said. 'We can't blunder about in the dark. Go back and tell Marino that, will you? Tell him we can play hush-hush as well as he can, but if he wants results quickly, we've got to know everything. And I don't care a damn what arrangement the Ambassador and the Assistant Commissioner or the Queen's High Admiral might come to. Use my car. I'll wait until the doctor arrives.'

'What's got into you?' she demanded.

'I ought to be on the telephone, ought to have told the Yard everything an hour ago, to warn all ports and airfields, all railway termini, every kicking-off point from England. The police ought to be on the look-out for the boy, have his description in every police station, in every newspaper. Tell Marino that.'

'And leave you alone with Shawn.'

'That's right,' Roger said.

'That won't do you any good,' she said. 'David Shawn won't talk to you about his work or anything that will lead up to it. You have a job to do too, Superintendent. You have to convince David that you can find the boy – that he doesn't have to start doing what the others tell him yet. Will you do that?'

'I will try,' Roger promised.

Obviously, he had to try.

He went to the front door with her, and she smiled and waved from his car as she settled down at the wheel. He fought the temptation to watch her until she was out of sight, turned, closed the front door with a snap, and hurried up the stairs. He tapped and went into the bedroom, without ceremony.

Belle Shawn lay in bed, the clothes drawn up to her neck, her face pale, her hair very tidy. Shawn was by the dressing-table, fully dressed, except for his coat and shoes, and was combing his thick, dark hair. He used Roger's trick, looking at the door in the mirror.

'Lissa said a doctor's coming,' he declared.

'He should be here,' said Roger. 'Did Mrs Meredith tell you that I am —'

'The man from Scotland Yard.' Shawn finished combing his hair, and turned round. His expression was blank, his lips were tightly set, betraying the way his teeth clenched, and his eyes still seemed to burn. He took his coat off the back of a chair, and began to put it on. 'The police are out,' he declared flatly. 'This is a private matter.'

'Keep it that way,' Roger said.

Shawn stopped moving, in surprise.

'If you don't care whether you see your son again or not,' Roger went on, 'keep it private.'

Shawn finished adjusting his coat, then moved slowly towards Roger. He was like a bear, massively powerful, but there was no clumsiness in his movements. His shoulders were bent, but he was still inches taller than Roger. His features seemed to grow bigger as he drew nearer. He moved his arms slowly, his great hands settled on Roger's shoulders. His fingers gripped, firmly, then gripped more tightly, as if he could crush the flesh and the bone. It hurt, but Roger didn't move, didn't flinch.

'You mean well,' Shawn said with great deliberation. 'But don't get in the way. I don't care what you say. I don't care what anyone says. This is not official. It isn't going to be official. I sent the boy away, understand. *I* sent him away.

I know where he is. I drugged his mother and myself, so that she couldn't prevent me, because I knew the boy was in danger. Understand that, Mr Scotland Yard? No one's been kidnapped, everything is just fine.'

5

THE OBSERVANT POLICEMAN

BUT for his eyes, Shawn could have been just a piece of sculpture hewn out of dark sandstone. His large features seemed more than life-size, and only his eyes were alive, telling of a man in anguish. The pressure of his fingers biting into Roger's shoulders grew stronger; like a killer's grip.

Roger said: 'So everything is fine.'

'You heard me.'

'All right,' said Roger. He tensed himself, then wrenched his shoulders free and backed away. Shawn didn't move after him. It came to his mind that Shawn would squeeze the life out of anyone who got in his way. Now, the man was in the grip of fierce passion roused by deadly hurt and deadlier fears; but he must always have the capacity for passion. 'All right,' repeated Roger. 'Now make your wife believe what you've told me.'

'Keep my wife out of this.'

'I'm not bringing her into it,' Roger retorted. 'She's already in. She wants her son back.'

Shawn raised his right hand, the fist clenched; he wanted to hit and to hurt.

'I'll look after my wife and my son,' he growled. 'You get out.'

The difficulty was for Roger to turn his back on the man, to overcome the fear that Shawn would strike at him when he did so. Roger stared into the stormy eyes, then turned slowly. Shawn didn't move. Roger reached the door, and for the first time since Shawn had started to speak, thought of other things; he realized for instance that while he had been in the bedroom, a car had drawn up outside. He opened the door.

Lissa Meredith stood at the head of the stairs. Her face was in shadow, but he caught the warning in her eyes; she didn't want Shawn to know that she was there. Probably she had overheard their conversation, returning quickly, anxious to know what he said to Shawn. Why should she be so anxious? Roger joined her, and they went downstairs together. A youthful-looking man with thin fair hair and a bulgy forehead stood in the hall. In his hand was a pigskin case. Lissa led the way to the dining-room, and they went in. She closed the door.

'Speak quietly,' she said. 'Mr West, this is Dr Fischer, Carl Fischer. Carl, you must handle David very carefully. Say I told you that Belle had collapsed, but you don't know another thing. Don't mention Ricky, don't let him think you know about that yet, just let him talk. And don't forget anything he says.'

Fischer gave a quick smile, splitting his face in two.

'As you say, honey. I'll go up.'

'Don't forget Fig Mayo,' Lissa said.

Fischer nodded and went out. Lissa turned to Roger and put a hand on his arm, lightly, naturally.

'You didn't go far,' Roger said heavily.

'I went to the nearest telephone and talked to Tony, and Carl arrived just after I got back. I heard everything David said, and I'm not surprised. I've always known that David would insist on doing what he believed best, whatever Belle thought. Until we get Ricky back, we can write David off.' The intensity of her manner, much more than her words, affected Roger. 'Do you want to do anything else here?'

'Not yet.'

They went to the front door and into the street. Roger's car was drawn up at the end of the cul-de-sac.

'Who is Fig Mayo?' Roger asked.

'Just a man who made David see red,' answered Lissa. 'He made a pass at Belle. He was drunk, or he wouldn't have asked for a suicide ticket. David threw him out of a fifth-floor window. Only a canvas canopy saved his life, all he broke was an arm and a leg. It was covered up as an accident, but it's the kind of accident that could happen again with David in certain moods.' She paused, and as they reached Roger's car she stated flatly: 'Fig Mayo is as big a man as you.'

'If Shawn threw me out of a fifth-floor window or even out of a door, we could put him in a cell and let him cool his heels,' Roger said. 'Think about that.'

Lissa put her head on one side and looked at him, half-smiling, wholly beautiful.

'It might be a good idea at that. What are you going to do now?'

'Talk to the policemen who were on duty here last night.'

'May I come?'

'But wouldn't you be more good here?'

'Carl can handle David – they're old friends. Carl can calm him down when he's raging with everyone else. Others from the Embassy will soon be here, too. Did you find out anything?' She was getting into the car.

'Whoever broke in almost certainly picked the lock of the back door,' said Roger, taking the wheel. 'So your orders are to keep as close to me as you can.'

'I like the idea, too! You're my first English detective, and it's quite an experience. There can't be many more like you.'

They didn't say much while Roger drove to the police station in Ealing. A uniformed constable was on duty outside, recognized Roger and came forward to open the door. He said good morning, and then saw Lissa Meredith; he looked quite startled.

It was hot in the sun, but cool inside the station, where a heavily-built and slow-speaking Superintendent talked for only a few minutes. They were soon in a small, barely-furnished room, where a middle-aged constable, helmet in hand, got up from an uncomfortable wooden chair. He had a large, florid face, a heavy greying moustache, greying hair and big, blue eyes, questioning eyes which suggested that he looked on the world during his nightly patrol in a state of perpetual wonderment touched with cynicism.

'This is Constable Maidment,' the Superintendent said. 'You don't mind if I leave you, West? Mrs Meredith.' He went out, and the door closed on him.

''Morning, Maidment.' Roger was brisk. 'Sorry to drag you out of bed.' Maidment had gone off duty at half past seven. 'This is Mrs Meredith, representing the American Embassy.' Maidment showed commendable self-control, his gaze only flickered over Lissa, then concentrated on Roger. 'Did you notice anything unusual in Wavertree Road during the night?'

PC Maidment was ready with his answer.

'Well, sir, in a way I did. In a *way* I didn't.'

'What happened?'

'It was about two o'clock, sir, or a little after. A car turned out of Wavertree Road and came towards me down Wickham Avenue. Don't often see a car I don't know at that hour, and it certainly wasn't any of the local doctors.' Roger recognized the officer who would tell a story better than he would answer questions, and gave him his head. 'Funny thing was the way I didn't hear the engine one minute, and the next I did. Very quiet around Wavertree Road at that hour, you can hear a cat move. Suddenly the engine started up and the head-lights went on, and the car was at the corner quick as snap.'

'Now what have you got up your sleeve?' demanded Roger.

Maidment beamed.

'Wavertree Road's on a *hill*, sir. Anyone starting from the top of the hill could switch off and then switch on again near the corner. So I took particular notice last night, and was extra careful trying front doors *and* back. I couldn't find anything wrong, sir. The car was a big Austin A70, one of those new jobs, very nice, and there aren't many about.'

'Sure of that?'

'Positive. Black. Might have been dark blue, only I don't think they do a blue one. Three men were in it, two at the front, one at the back – I saw them as they passed beneath a lamp. It wasn't going fast, not really fast. The man at the back looked round after me, I could see his face when it went under the lamp.' Caution tempered his eagerness. 'Not that I could recognize it again, sir.'

'And this was about two o'clock?'

'Near as dammit, sir.'

'Anything else?'

'Everything was quiet and normal,' answered PC Maidment, and actually looked uneasy. 'I hope nothing went wrong I didn't catch on to, sir.'

'Nothing you could be blamed for. Are you sure there were only three men in the car?'

'I only *saw* three.'

'Good,' said Roger. 'Is all of this in your report?'

'Yes, sir.'

'Well, keep it all under your hat, Maidment. There may have been a bit of funny business last night, if there was we don't want the people involved to know we're suspicious. All clear?'

'Quite clear, sir.'

'Now make up on your beauty sleep.' Roger nodded and smiled, and opened the door for Lissa to precede him into the passage. He led the way to the Superintendent's office, which was empty. 'Sit down a minute,' he said, and went across to the Superintendent's wooden armchair, sat at the tidy desk, was careful not to disturb four piles of papers, and lifted the telephone.

'Chief Inspector Sloan, please . . . Hallo, Bill. A black Austin A70, one of the new models, left Wavertree Road, Ealing, about two o'clock this morning. Check its movements where you can, will you?'

'Right.'

'There's a possibility that it was heading for London Airport,' Roger went on. 'Check that first. Check what aircraft left London Airport after three o'clock, and find out whether a ten-year-old boy was on board any of them.'

'Heading where?'

'America, probably, but that's a guess. Even if you don't get a line at London, try Gatwick and the smaller airfields. Give this absolute priority.'

'Right! What does the boy look like?'

'I haven't a description yet, but probably small for his age. And Bill, if you get anything, call me at the American Embassy. Ask for Mr Marino, and if I'm not with him, I'll call you as soon as I get there.'

'What *is* all this?' demanded Sloan.

'When I know I'll tell you,' Roger said. ''Bye.'

Lissa had a half-smoked Pall Mall between her lips, and as Roger opened his case, she leaned forward with a lighter. She looked at him above the flame, and it went out as he saw the smile in her eyes.

'So you think he's been flown back home.'

'It could be.'

'How is that machine you call a mind working?'

'You want David Shawn in England on a special assignment, on work he can't do in the States. His wife wants to be there anyhow, and he doesn't want an estrangement with his wife. So already he has plenty of reason for thinking that he would be happier back home. If some third party wants to stop him working, and that's what you and Marino have implied, a good way of doing this would be to tell him that his son is safe in the States. That would be one means of stopping him staying in England.' Roger glanced at his watch. 'Now it's nearly one o'clock. If we really want to work fast, we ought to telephone Kennedy Airport, and find out whether a boy passenger reaches there from England. It's about a twelve-hour flight, they couldn't have left before three o'clock, so we've an hour or so in hand. Care to telephone Marino?'

'You call him,' Lissa said.

'Will he be at lunch?'

'He doesn't go out to lunch, he has a sandwich in the office.'

Marino was a careful listener, and did not ask for anything to be repeated. The name of Ricky Shawn wasn't mentioned, but Marino promised to call Kennedy Airport at once, and rang off.

'And now what?' Lissa asked; there was a hint of mockery in her voice.

'Do you think the Embassy could find a sandwich for us, too?'

'It could run to a good lunch, after you've talked to Tony again, and you and I could discuss the weather.'

'Wonderful idea,' said Roger dryly. 'But I'm just a working man, and probably there was some other crime in London last night. Another time.'

'There may not be another time. If David goes back to New York, I shall be sent after him.'

'If he's so important, you can find a way to stop him,' Roger said. 'At least until there's time to look for his son. If you keep Shawn and his wife apart, it might help. Deal with them singly.' He laughed, as a kind of foreboding swept over him, but he didn't try to put it into words. 'I always talked too much.'

He stood up, and they went downstairs, out into the heat of this fierce September day, and drove fast to Grosvenor Square.

Lissa led the way into Marino's office, where Marino still sat at his huge desk, as if he hadn't moved since they had left. But his smile had none of the easy amiability of the morning; it was tense enough to make Lissa stand still, half-way across the room.

'What's happened?' she demanded.

Marino said: 'Sit down, Superintendent. If you'd been sitting here when it first started, instead of me, maybe we would have found Ricky by now. I don't understand why I didn't guess they would ship him back to the States by air. I can't think why you didn't, Lissa. Ricky was on a 'plane which left London Airport at three-fifteen this morning. But he didn't go on to New York, he was taken off at Gander. He could be anywhere in Canada by now. He could be anywhere,' he repeated. 'I've got the FBI chasing for news of him, but you know how difficult it will be to find him in Canada or the States. We've lost that boy, and we could have saved him. The only hope of quick results is from this end. Can you act as fast as you can think, Superintendent?'

'Let me talk to the Yard,' Roger said.

6

OWNER OF AN AUSTIN

SLOAN had already found that a boy, the only child on the TSR 10, had left London in the company of a middle-aged man who had an American passport in the name of McMahon; the boy had travelled with a passport under the name of Sims. The child had seemed sleepy, McMahon had fussed him a great deal, no one had suspected there was anything wrong. Descriptions of McMahon varied, but three different reports from the airport had one thing in common. He had a big head: big that was in proportion to his body.

They had arrived at London Airport in an old Buick, the driver had gone off with the car as soon as he had set down his passengers. Sloan was already trying to trace the Buick. The Austin A70 had been traced as far as Hammersmith, and the Hammersmith police were already checking on all A70s garaged in the district.

Roger told Marino and Lissa Meredith this while they were still in Marino's office.

'You have to find the owner of that car,' Marino said flatly. 'West, you don't know how important that is.'

Lissa said: 'Could it be the time for telling him *how* important?'

Marino said slowly: 'Maybe.'

But he didn't go on for a long time; it seemed a long time. He watched Roger, steadily, piercingly.

'I guess you're right,' he said at last. 'That's been agreed with the Ambassador. West, here's the story. David Shawn has spent a great deal of time in Russia and France during the Test Ban discussions. He is a key man because as a scientist he is believed to have discovered a way of checking even the smaller nuclear explosions. Russia, France and China all want one of two things, if not both; to prevent the United States from having this detector, or to obtain it themselves and so neutralize its value. Either way, they need him. I can tell you that the wires have been humming between here and Washington this morning, it's that important.'

'I can see how important,' Roger said.

'I'm sure you do. There are other things you should know. When in his Connecticut home last spring, Shawn was shot at. He was nearly run down by an auto two months later.

Since then, the FBI has been watching him closely, because we've expected more trouble, and this is it.' Marino paused, then turned towards Lissa. 'Carl Fischer says that David is at his worst.'

'He looked like doing a Fig Mayo on Mr West,' Lissa said dryly. 'How is Belle?'

'Carl gave her a shot, so there won't be any trouble with her for the next twenty-four hours. David approved. He doesn't want trouble any more than the rest of us – not more trouble than he can help, anyway. But we don't need to hide anything from ourselves. David won't be any use to us or anyone until the boy's found. Belle will blame him, and that will make him just a bag of nerves. West —' Marino paused, a smile thawed the bleakness of his face. 'The hell with West! Roger, David Shawn's mind has been on a knife edge between sanity and insanity for a long time. It's partly the strain of his work, and believe me, that's a strain enough for a dozen men. He lives his part, he's a man of two distinct personalities – some say schizophrenic. On vacation, or when he's not working on some new angle, he's liable to do crazy things – call that a safety valve. When he's working, the work seems to absorb the spare energy, and he's near normal – until a crisis arises. And this is a *crisis*. At a time like this he won't listen to reason.'

'He might, if you started to get tough with him,' Roger said. 'He throws a man out of a window, and it's all hushed up. He's doing a vital job over here, and he delivers an ultimatum – bring his wife, or he won't do it. Next time you had to bring his son over. You've built him up so that he thinks he's the only man who can do this job.'

Marino said softly: 'I guess he is.'

'Why not try making him think he isn't?'

'He'd throw his hand in.'

'There's a risk of that anyhow,' Roger argued. 'You can't seriously think that after this, he'll be satisfied to stay here.

You might get the son back for him, but you'll never convince him that it won't happen again. He might say he will stay, hoping it will make you work harder to find the boy, but afterwards —' He shrugged. 'He could turn sour on you. But he looks to me like a man with the inevitable weak link – his pride. If his supremacy in his field is threatened, it might change his outlook.'

There was silence.

Marino rubbed his black stubble; he already needed a shave.

'The tame psychiatrist,' he said musingly. 'What do you think, Lissa?'

'I wouldn't like to be the one to tell David he's got a rival.'

'How would you start going about it?' Marino asked Roger.

'Give him another shock. Next time he starts throwing his weight about, fall on him like a ton of bricks. Stop making him think that he can get away with murder.'

Marino said slowly: 'It's certainly worth thinking about. Any more ideas?'

'Shawn's wife,' Roger said. 'Is anyone getting at her? She's a neurotic —'

'Who said so?'

'I implied it,' Lissa put in. 'I didn't mean that a psychiatrist would say so.'

'We've tried that angle,' Marino said. 'She isn't neurotic in the true sense. Losing her own money hurt her pride, and maybe held her to Shawn, that's all. She doesn't take drugs. She's just a woman who's so full up with self-pity she's made herself a nervous wreck.'

'Does she know how important Shawn's work is?'

'She doesn't know what it is,' said Marino, 'but she knows only the big time would have kept him in Europe when she wanted him home.'

The telephone bell rang, and Marino picked up the receiver. 'Yes, Herb? . . . Put him through.' He held the receiver out to Roger. 'Mr Hardy, for you.'

Roger took the telephone; suddenly realizing that it was the Assistant Commissioner, and that it was in his power to move him from this job, which might be handled better by a MI5 agent, or a Special Branch man. He had not until now known how important it was to him that he should see this job through.

Marino and Lissa were watching him intently.

'Hallo, Handsome.' Hardy was in an affable mood. 'You are assigned to the American Embassy for the time being to do whatever they ask. If you come up against anything you think you shouldn't do, get through to me, but don't lose any time about it.'

'Not a moment, sir!'

'If you need help, use Sloan.'

'I will,' said Roger.

'Any hope of an early result?' Hardy asked. 'It's not just important, it's vital. Work day and night, but get results.'

'There's a half-chance,' Roger said. 'Thanks, Mr Hardy.'

'And listen,' said Hardy. 'Don't tell Janet or anyone where you're working, keep it under your hat and keep your hat on all the time.'

'Right.'

'Luck,' said Hardy, laconically.

Roger put down the receiver, pursed his lips, and then looked into Marino's eyes. He was acutely aware of the way Lissa looked at him.

He said: 'I'm under your orders.'

'You aren't under anyone's orders,' Marino retorted at once. 'Where it's a case of getting Ricky back, or finding out where he is, we'll take yours. But you can't work if you're hungry. Lissa, why don't you go and get Roger some lunch?'

• • •

Sitting opposite Lissa Meredith, eating a huge T-bone steak, the urgency of the Shawn kidnapping seemed to fade. It wasn't anything she said or did; it wasn't even the radiance in her face, a glow from some inner fire which certainly hadn't been lighted by him. It was simply that, being with Lissa Meredith, there wasn't room for anything else; not unless she wanted it. It was like being cut off from the world. Roger knew that it wouldn't last, wasn't sure that he wanted it to. He wasn't sure of anything, except that it was as much for her as for any official reason that he wanted to break this case open; to find a child who was with a man known as McMahon somewhere in Canada or the United States.

It didn't even occur to him that there wasn't a chance.

A waiter was pouring out coffee, when another waiter came up with a telephone, which he plugged into the wall.

'For Superintendent West.'

'Thanks,' said Roger.

'Roger,' said Bill Sloan, a moment later. He wasn't breathless, but a note of urgency was in his voice; the world came back, the problem appeared in sharp outline again. 'I think we're on to something.'

'The car?' asked Roger sharply.

'It might be. Peel got on to it at a garage near Hammersmith Broadway – just off the Fulham Palace Road. An Austin A70, and an American took it in a week ago, with big-end trouble. The same man collected it.' He paused. 'Peel found out that the car came from the Barnes direction and went back the same way. Two or three garages on the Barnes Road have supplied petrol to an A70 with an American driver. Is it all right to ask the Barnes police to see what they can do?'

'Yes, and don't lose any time. Send Peel to Barnes.'

'He's there already.'

'Fine. Then meet me at Hammersmith Underground, by the main bookstall, in half an hour,' Roger said.

'This time I'm glad to let you go,' Lissa told him.

• • •

Sloan, looking even bigger than usual in a brown suit that was a shade too small, stood by the magazines and books displayed on the stall at the underground station. He didn't look round until Roger was within a yard of him. They moved off together, mixing with the crowd which had come off a train, turned left at the side entrance to the station, walking quickly, but without seeming to hurry, to Roger's parked car.

'Follow me at a good distance,' Roger said. 'Not towards the garage, we can tackle that afterwards. Come on to the Divisional HQ and I'll meet you there.'

Sloan said: 'What's on?'

'It looks as if we're being watched by a man behind the taxi outside the station.' Neither of the policemen looked round. 'He's been watching me, I think.'

Sloan grinned, as if at some joke.

'Be seeing you!' He went towards his own car.

Roger took a newspaper from the seat of his, then slammed the door and walked in the other direction. He passed the man near the taxi without glancing at him, waited at a pedestrian crossing until the lights changed, then walked briskly to the other side of the road. He nearly blundered into a man coming towards him, apologized, side-stepped, and faced the opposite pavement for the second he needed. The man was showing obvious interest. Roger hurried, turned into Glenthorne Road and glanced round.

The man stepped on to a pedestrian crossing, tall, thin, wearing a raincoat; and it was much too hot for any kind of coat. He hurried. Roger slowed down, giving the other man plenty of time to catch up with him. The man walked by without a glance, then went into a shop doorway.

He came out when Roger had passed it.

7

DEAD MAN

ROGER turned into the entrance of the Hammersmith police station, was recognized, nodded and hurried to the Superintendent's office. Wirral, in command at Hammersmith, was a lanky, melancholy Yorkshireman, slow of movement and speech but quick enough on the uptake.

'I'm really in a hurry,' Roger said. 'There's a man outside.' He described the man in the raincoat. 'Have him tailed, will you?'

Wirral said: 'Right away,' lifted a telephone and gave instructions to someone named 'George'. Then he said: 'What?' and listened, grunted and rang off.

'The man has been hanging about for an hour or more, the sergeant downstairs noticed him. Seemed interested in this station and the Underground. What's it all about, Handsome?'

Roger grinned. 'Secret list, this time. Had anything on the go around here? Big enough to bring Bill Sloan and me to have a look round, and the raincoat to want to find out if there's a big show on?'

'We've got a body,' Wirral said, looking more melancholy than ever; but his eyes held a smile. 'Is that big enough? Cut throat.'

'Suicide?'

'Four inch gash, carotid severed, much more and it would have been decapitation. He was taken out of the river a couple of hours ago. When I saw your pretty face I thought you'd come about it.'

'Where's the body?'

'It ought to be in the morgue by now.' Wirral used the telephone again and spoke to an echo that came from the receiver. 'Where's the stiff we took out of the Thames? . . . It is, good man.' He rang off. 'Just arrived at the morgue. Like to have a look?'

'Yes, thanks. Get someone to talk about a body in the river – in the hearing of my man in the raincoat, will you?'

Wirral eyed him thoughtfully; warily.

'You look as if you want to cut someone's throat yourself.' The telephone bell rang. 'Superintendent Wirral . . . It's Sloan,' he said to Roger. 'Downstairs.'

'Ask him to wait.'

'He's probably a better tailer than the man I've put on to your raincoat.'

'But he's known to the raincoat.'

Wirral shrugged. 'We'll be down, Bill,' he said into the mouthpiece, and rang off.

On the way to the front hall he asked about Janet and the boys; the West family were known to most London police. Roger answered mechanically, letting his thoughts run now that he had digested the facts. He had not been followed to Hammersmith; the man in the raincoat had been here, and knew him. Wirral's George had better be good. If the man in the raincoat discovered that he was being followed, he would slip his man, and he would also know that he was suspect.

'How good is George?' Roger asked.

'As good as I've got.'

'I hope you train 'em well.'

Drawing up with Sloan, Roger told him what had happened, and where they were going, and they walked together to the morgue, all big, tall men, all talking earnestly. The man in the raincoat was on the other side of the road, at a bus-stop; he had an evening newspaper folded in front of him, and seemed to be reading it. Two men walked from the police station to the bus-stop, and stood waiting and talking; laughing. One of them pointed to Roger.

'He's letting the raincoat hear that we asked for you,' Wirral said.

'Thanks,' said Roger briefly. 'Sorry I'm making so much mystery. Is there a back way out of the morgue?'

'Yes.'

'That's for us,' Roger said to Sloan. 'I'll go first, and – no I won't. Wirral, call me anything you like, but do something else for me, will you? Have one of your boys go to – what's the name of the garage, Bill?'

'Stebber's.'

'I know Stebber's,' Wirral said. 'And what?'

'Find out if anyone has been watching the garage today.'

They had reached the doorway of the morgue.

'I'll go and lay things on,' said Wirral. 'Hang on until I get there, and I'll give you the latest on the raincoat.'

He doubled back, and Roger and Sloan went into the small outer room at the morgue, then into the chill, bleak room itself. The stone slabs were empty, except for one in a corner on which lay a body partly covered by a sheet. Three men were working close by. One of the men, a police photographer, was taking his last picture before packing up his equipment. The second man was going through the dead man's pockets, handing everything he found to the third, who made a pencilled note of it before laying it down. The searcher had a sodden wallet in his hand.

'One billfold,' he said. Looking up, he recognized Roger, and at once stopped being casual and looking careless. 'Afternoon, sir!'

Roger smiled. 'Hallo. Why billfold?'

'It's American.' The man handed the wallet over. 'Some dollars in it, too.' He watched Roger take it, pull some wet dollar bills out and look at the corners.

'Twenties,' Roger said, and counted. 'Seven twenties,

two or three tens – count it all, will you?'

Nothing in his voice reflected the surge of excitement he felt, and Sloan schooled himself to show no unusual interest. Roger went to the slab which was being used as a table and looked through the oddments already on it. A sodden handkerchief, keys and a small knife on a chain, a small reel of Scotch tape, three credit cards, common in the United States, little known in England. They showed the name of Ed Scammel.

He took them to the searcher.

'Where did you find these?'

'Funny thing,' the man said. 'You'd expect them to be in his wallet, wouldn't you? They weren't, though. The lining of his pocket was torn, these were inside the lining. I was just checking the unlikely places first.'

'Good,' said Roger. 'Sergeant – what's your name?'

'Day, sir.'

'Day, don't tell anyone this man was probably an American. Don't tell the others in the office, just have it on record he's not identified yet but there's nothing unusual about him. Clear?'

There was a chorus of 'yes, sirs'.

'Thanks.' Roger examined everything taken from the dead man's pockets, but nothing seemed to offer help.

The door opened, and Wirral came in, lowering his head to miss the lintel. Roger and Sloan went across to him. For a few moments they stayed near the door, while the others continued to work, shooting curious glances towards them.

'Raincoat took a taxi, George got another,' he said. 'You satisfied him, I should think. I'll have word from Stebber's Garage in ten minutes or so.'

'Fine,' said Roger, and smiled, trying to relax; but he couldn't.

He had, in fact, been unable to relax since the moment he had heard that the child had been kidnapped. The kidnapping had tied a knot in his vitals, and everything else had drawn the knot tighter; even Lissa Meredith. Now, he wanted evidence of an association between the American found in the Thames with his throat slashed, the missing child, the Austin A70 with the American driver, and the Buick which had been seen at London Airport. Kidnapping was always vicious, standing out wickedly among crimes, the work of criminals without feeling, ruthless, deadly. Like the murder of the man whose credit cards named him as Ed Scammel, of Elizabeth, New Jersey. Behind all that was the atmosphere Marino and Lissa had created. From being relaxed to a point of boredom on his way to the Yard that morning, he had become as taut as a wire rope: a thin wire rope.

'Fine,' he repeated. 'Wirral, I've asked these chaps not to mention that the dead man is American. That really matters, for an hour or so. Fix it, will you?' He hardly gave Wirral time to nod. 'Will you have everything found in his pockets packed up and taken to the Yard right away? Marked for me, to go into Hardy's office.' That was the one way he could make sure that no one blundered.

'Yes,' said Wirral. 'What else?'

Roger grinned.

'How soon can I have a picture of the chap?'

'I'll have one rushed through,' Wirral promised.

'Get plenty done, we might need 'em soon,' Roger said.

Ten minutes later, they were back at the police station. The message from Stebber's Garage had arrived: no one had been seen hanging about the garage, it had been just another day, except for Peel's inquiries about the Austin A70.

The wet print came up quicker than Roger had expected. He put it between a fold of blotting-paper before going out.

Stebber's was just another garage, small, untidy, reeking of petrol and oil, with two youths and a mechanic in dirty overalls, one at a bench, two with their faces buried in the engine of a fifteen-year-old car. There was the usual hoist on its thick, greased pole; the steady beat of an engine charging accumulators and batteries made a monotonous song. Stebber was a little plump man in a stained grey suit, who came hurrying from a small office, glass walled on three sides. He had a pencil behind his right ear, grubby fat cheeks creased in a smile that was probably more anxious than it looked. He rubbed his hands together.

'What can I do for you, gents?'

Roger showed his card. 'About this American and the Austin A70 – did he give you an address?'

'No, sir, he didn't,' said Stebber, and now the anxiety showed through. 'Not that there was any need,' he added defensively. 'Just wanted the job done quick. There's no law that says —'

'Had you seen the man before?'

'No, and I ain't seen him since. I've answered all these questions once, and —'

'I'm just checking up,' Roger said.

'Stolen, was it?'

'We'd like to find it,' Roger temporized. 'Any special characteristics, did you notice?'

'No, *I* didn't, but Bert, that's the mechanic who did the job, wasn't in when the other cop – the other 'tec come, *he* noticed something. Not certain, mind you, but the Austin A70 might have been fitted with false number plates, some time.'

'Only *might*? Where's that mechanic?'

'Bert!' bellowed Stebber.

Bert was in dingy white overalls and a new trilby hat with a few oily fingermarks on the brim. He had seen cars fitted to take two or three number plates – examined them for the police, he explained – and this Austin might have been fitted for that, but there had been only one number plate.

'Did you give the other officer the number?' asked Roger.

'Certainly,' Stebber said. 'Help the police in every way I can, that's my motto.'

'Keep to it. By the way,' Roger said, taking the fold of blotting paper from under his arm, and unfolding it, 'have either of you ever seen this chap?'

They stared at the photograph.

'Why, that's the Yank!' Stebber exclaimed. 'That's him! Ain't it, Bert?'

'You couldn't mistake a face like that, could you?' Bert asked.

• • •

Armed with a dozen prints of the American's photograph, Roger drove to Barnes police station, where Peel was collecting more garage reports. They had the names of three garages where an American with an A70 had called for petrol.

The photograph was recognized at all of them.

'So the car's home is about here somewhere,' Detective Inspector Peel said. He was another, younger, Sloan; fresh complexion, blue eyes, short fair hair.

'We want it, and we want it in a hurry,' Roger said. 'And we don't want the owner to know we've traced it. I'm going to the Yard, to get everything laid on. You'll be in charge down here.'

'We'll find it,' Peel said.

Sloan was at the Yard, with fresh news; the registration number given by Stebber's Garage for the A70 was a false one, there was no such number registered anywhere in England. He had sent six Yard men down to Barnes straight away, but they had found nothing. Even the man in the raincoat had shaken off Wirral's George.

• • •

At half past ten the next morning, Roger finished a

telephone talk with Marino, and Lissa. There was no news of importance about the Shawns; no real change in the condition of either.

At ten forty-five, Peel called through from Barnes.

'I think we've got something, sir. Can you come down?'

'As fast as I can get there,' promised Roger. 'Found either of the cars?'

'I haven't *seen* it, but the Austin is kept by a woman named Norwood – Mrs Clarice Norwood – in a house called 'Rest', on the riverside near Chiswick Steps. The dead American has been seen to drive it to her house. She left for Paris, forty-eight hours ago, and the place has been empty since, according to the tradespeople.'

'Have it checked, fast, but leave the garage to me,' said Roger. 'Wait a minute! The Norwood woman – what can you tell me about her?'

Peel said: 'She's a gay widow. Used to have a lot of men friends, but recently she's been faithful to one.'

'Name?'

'I've only heard about this in the last hour,' Peel protested.

'Put the other men on to tracing Mrs Norwood and trying to get something about the regular boyfriend,' Roger ordered. 'This could be very important indeed.'

8

GISSING

THE brick house was small, pleasant, secluded, and the garden ran down to the sluggish Thames. Across the river were the dark-red walls of factories; above and below the house were jetties, warehouses and hustle. Here was an oasis, protected by beech trees in full green dress on three sides, by the river on the fourth. There was a small lawn, with a few rose bushes standing in freshly turned beds, surrounded by closely growing shrubs. A wooden jetty stood out from the river bank, a white-painted dinghy tied alongside, swaying gently. Most of the windows faced the river; those looking on to the beech trees were small.

It was after twelve o'clock noon. The house had been visited by a Yard man, posing as an Electricity Board official, but no one had answered his knock.

Across the river, at the window of a warehouse, Sloan was standing with a pair of powerful binoculars. Two other detectives also watched, too far away to be of help if help were needed, but near enough to observe all comings and goings to the house, which had no number, just the name: 'Rest'. The porch was covered with pale-green tiles, the front door and all the woodwork were of light brown, green tiles covered the gabled roof.

The garage was at the back of the house.

Roger drove along the narrow road leading to 'Rest', passed the beech trees and felt cut off from everyone as he drew up to the white garage doors.

There was ample room for the Austin, which was bigger than most made in England. The electric light and back daylight shone on the glossy black bodywork, the sleek lines. Roger opened the driving-door, sat at the wheel, looked in all the pockets and the glove compartment. Then he got busy, searching for prints. It took him five minutes to make sure that the car had been cleaned up thoroughly. Later, there could be an inch-by-inch examination; now, he had more urgent work to do.

He went out of the garage, turned his own car and approached the house. The only sound was the lapping of water nearby, the chirping of birds. From the house, silence. He studied the back door, and tried the handle. It was locked.

He walked round the house on crazy paving, neatly laid,

no trap for careless feet. The lapping of the water grew louder. The sun shone bright on the rippling river. He reached the front door, and knocked sharply; after a pause he knocked again, then rang the bell.

He glanced over his shoulder.

No one was in sight; no one had been in sight since he had left Peel two hundred yards away where this little private road led off the main highway. Peel had wanted to come with him; would have followed, if he hadn't received strict instructions to stay put. Had that been safe? Was *he* safe? Did the trees conceal watchers, men who would slit another's throat?

Roger tried the handle, but this door was also locked. He walked to the nearest window; examined it, and discovered that it would not be easy to force. If all the windows were the same, he might have to break one in order to get inside. He had no search warrant, but Hardy would cover him for that.

Retracing his steps round the house, he tried a skeleton key in the back door; after a lot of twisting and turning, it worked, but he found that the door was bolted. Close by, he found a small window with a fastener he could reach with a long nail file. In five minutes he climbed into the kitchen. There was no sound. He shut the window and walked slowly across to a door leading into a square hall; there was no passage, only three other rooms, two on the right, one on the left; and a flight of stairs, carpeted from wall to banisters; the hall floor was also covered by a fitted carpet. His footsteps were muffled by dark-fawn pile. He went straight to the front door, unbolted and opened it and stood for a moment on the porch, not waving, but making sure that Sloan had time to see him. Then he closed the door and went inside again.

The three downstairs rooms were bright, airy and pleasant; there was nothing striking about them or the furniture. Homely but well-to-do folk lived here. On a baby grand piano were several photographs, all of the same woman; an attractive woman whose pictures here ranged over fifteen to twenty years. There was no photograph of a man.

Roger went upstairs, the only sound the faint rub of his clothes, cloth on cloth, and his soft footfalls. He found himself whistling softly, under his breath. This was exactly as he had expected, but there was something else: his own mood of expectancy. Fearful expectancy?

There were four bedrooms, two bathrooms; all were spotless but for a light dust, comfortable, pleasantly furnished in a bleak modern way, all empty. Yet two of the bedrooms had the air of being lived in. A woman's coat lay over the back of a chair, a piece of tissue, dabbed with lipstick, was in a small wastepaper basket, together with a twist or two of blonde hair. There were more pictures of the same woman, but once again Roger could see no photograph of a man. He began searching the bedrooms, twenty wasted minutes irritating him.

There were no men's clothes in any wardrobe, no shaving-gear, no tell-tale oddments. They could have been taken away, Roger mused, but more likely no man lived here, only Mrs Norwood.

An hour after he had arrived he drove off. The only thing he took away was an impression of a key, in soap, of the back door. This door he left locked; but he was careful to pull back the bolt which secured the door on the inside.

• • •

From the Yard, Roger telephoned the *Sureté Nationale*; a Paris acquaintance was quick to understand and to promise to look for Mrs Norwood, but not to let her know she was being watched. Unfortunately, it might be days before a Paris report came through – and Ricky Shawn was in the hands of murderers.

Roger had full local reports on what little was known about the woman and several conflicting descriptions of her regular boyfriend; all agreed on one thing only – that he was middle-aged.

After three o'clock that afternoon, when the telephone rang, he was ready for anything – except a call from Paris. A French Inspector, with good English, was in triumphant mood.

'This Mrs Norwood, Superintendent. I think we have found her.'

Roger's heart leapt.

'Wonderful!' It was almost too good to be true.

'It is not so bad, you admit. She answers the description you gave me. She gives her true name. She is at the Hotel de Paris, on the Boulevard Madeleine. Also, she has been there before. We have *seen* her before.'

Roger said tensely: 'Go on.'

'We questioned the man who was then with her. A Mr Jack Gissing. Gissing.' The Frenchman spelt the name out carefully. 'At the time, we asked you for information about this man. It was three – no, four months ago. You will have a record, perhaps?'

'We'll have a record!' The breaks always came when they were least expected. 'I can't say thanks enough,' Roger said, fighting down excitement.

Very soon, he was going through the records of a man who was known as Gissing, a wealthy man of independent means. Nothing was known against him except that he had some mysterious way of outwitting most currency regulations. It was surprising how little had been learned about him. The French had suspected him of smuggling, but had been able to prove nothing.

Roger sent for the Sergeant who had made the inquiries, a dark-haired, chunky Cornishman, who had interviewed Gissing on his return to England. The man had been living in a luxury service flat in Kensington, his passport had been in order, he had seemed amused by the investigation. What was he like? Not a man one would forget, but one difficult to describe. Not big, not small.

'We want the Home Office files for his passport photograph,' Roger said. 'You'd better go for it – I'll phone 'em.'

It took time.

Marino telephoned, Roger promised news of a kind soon, and rang off. Had he been too abrupt? Much more abrupt than he would have been if Lissa had telephoned. He read the report on Gissing until he knew it off by heart; another case of a man of whom practically nothing was known, a vague past, an equally vague source of income. He did some buying and selling on the 'Change, had some overseas balances which were blocked; no known American income or capital.

The Sergeant came back, as nearly flurried as a Cornishman could be.

'If that's Jack Gissing, I'm a Chinaman,' he said, handing the passport photograph to Roger. 'He *might* just pass with a photo like that, but more likely he changed the one on his passport. That won't help with the Press, will it?'

'It won't help with anything or anyone,' Roger said. 'We'll have to work on your description.'

Sloan took over, to send the description to ports and airfields in the hope that Gissing would be recognized. Roger, less buoyant, went to Grosvenor Square.

Herb had gone home. Lissa wasn't there, but her presence seemed to linger. If Marino had been conscious of any telephone brusqueness, he had not let it worry him.

It was nearly seven o'clock.

'Hi, Roger,' Marino said, and waved to a chair. 'You'll have a drink, I know.' There was a tray on his desk, with Scotch whisky, rye, a gleaming cocktail shaker, a bowl of ice, salted almonds, pecan, cashews and peanuts. 'What will it be?'

'Whisky and soda, please,' Roger said.

Marino poured the drinks from where he sat, stretching out his long arms, hardly leaning to the right or left; it was almost as if he couldn't move his body. His big face had an amiable look, here was a man it seemed nothing could really ruffle – yet the kidnapping of Ricky Shawn had ruffled him. The cut of his grey coat was faultless.

He poured rye on to ice, for himself.

'Here's to Scotland Yard,' he said, and drank. His eyes smiled. 'So it hasn't gone the way you hoped.'

'Not all thc way,' Roger said, 'but we've found the A70 used at Ealing, and other things have developed.' Marino went tense, and Roger told him exactly what he now knew, going on: 'Much depends on how far Gissing was responsible for the kidnapping. I think we'll catch up with him. There's a chance that he'll use the house by the river – else why send his light o' love away. We're having it watched. If Gissing knows where the boy is, we'll find a way of making him talk. Perhaps we can use the murder of Ed Scammel as a lever. Know anything about Scammel?'

Marino said: 'I called Washington. If they get a line on him, they'll call back.'

'Good. If Gissing thinks he'll have to face a murder charge, he'll probably talk fast enough.'

'Could be, too. How long has Ed Scammel worked for Gissing?'

'At least three months. He has been seen driving the Austin around Barnes and Hammersmith at intervals for that period. We're trying to find out who else Ed mixed with over here. He's known to have had lunch once or twice a week with another American in a café at Hammersmith. The other man's name takes some believing. It's Jaybird.'

Marino smiled. 'You'll put the L in for him.'

'With luck, we'll have some news about him tonight,' said Roger. 'But we can't hide the fact that we're looking for an American citizen. The fact that one was murdered hasn't leaked out yet – officially, the body's not identified. But there are limits to how much we can keep secret. I told you that on the telephone. I don't think we ought to keep it all from the Press – or try to.'

'I said, use your own judgment,' Marino reminded him. 'Keep doing that, and I'll be happy. The thing I want is to hold the newspapermen off Shawn. That means keeping the kidnapping out of the newspapers. Can you do this?'

Roger said reluctantly: 'So far, we have. The neighbour was satisfied without much trouble. Officially, Ricky Shawn has been sent into the country – neighbours won't be surprised that he doesn't show up in Wavertree Road. Officially there was a burglary at Number Thirty-one the night before last – nothing much stolen. It will get a paragraph or two in the local newspapers, but nothing in the daily Press.' Roger finished his drink, thought he heard a sound at the door, looked round and was disappointed. 'What news have you got for me?'

'Nothing from the States,' Marino said. 'Belle Shawn is still under Carl's sedation. Shawn hasn't left his house. I asked him to come and see me, but he refused. Don't tell me about Mahomet and the mountain.' Marino was still urbane, had himself under much stricter control than the previous morning. 'Shawn wants to pack up and go home as soon as Belle is fit to travel.'

'No more messages?'

'We haven't intercepted any on the telephone,' said Marino, 'but one might have reached him, telling him to go back to the States if he wants to see the boy again.'

'Will you let him?'

'If Shawn goes home, we'll never get him back – and we need him here.'

'Is that an answer?'

'We don't want to have to keep him against his will. We want him to co-operate freely. There just isn't a way of making a man do what he doesn't wish to do, Roger – not if you want him to put all he's got into doing it. You suggested the line we should take with him, and maybe we will, but whatever line we take, it won't alter basic facts. You're right in this way: even if we get Ricky back, Shawn will still think of future danger, so to hold him, we have to get the boy back and also convince Shawn there's nothing waiting for him round the corner.'

Roger said slowly: 'I can't tell you why I don't like Shawn. I just don't. Perhaps it's because you're so concerned with him that you forget the other trifle.'

Marino looked his question.

'A ten-year-old boy, highly strung, used to having life made easy, was last known to be with McMahon, who probably slit Ed Scammel's throat.'

'That's right,' Marino said slowly. 'First things first. To me, to a lot of other people, that boy isn't vital because he's a child having a hell of a time, only because of his influence on his father. So I'm cold-blooded. But does it make any difference? You want to get him back because he's a boy, I want him back just as badly because he's the son of his father. I held out on you about the reason for Shawn's importance, because I had to. But you're holding out on me for a reason I don't know.'

Marino was quick; very quick.

'What makes you think so?'

'It just occurred to me, I guess. And to Lissa. It occurred to Lissa first. She said that she didn't believe that you'd told us everything you'd been thinking. Lissa thinks you're good, Roger – more than good, she thinks you're red-hot. She says you've a mind that jumps twice as fast and twice as high as the next man, and being English, you don't talk much. I've known her for a long time, and she isn't often wrong. What are you keeping to yourself?'

Marino spoke amiably enough; and waited patiently for an answer.

'A guess,' Roger said, and stood up. He glanced towards the door again, but it didn't open; Lissa wasn't coming. 'We know that a child was taken to Gander early yesterday morning, we know he was small for his age and thin, we don't know that it was Ricky Shawn. It could have been a stooge. You, everyone in the hunt, would jump to the States as the likely place for them to take the boy. Gissing, or McMahon, or unknowns, would know which way we'd jump, give us plenty to jump after, and plant the boy somewhere else. With Mrs Clarice Norwood in Paris, perhaps. Or somewhere in England. We're still getting reports at the Yard of all the boys around that age who left the country from three a.m. yesterday morning, and we could be fooled even if we do get word of them, because they could have dressed Ricky as a girl.

'Tony, you've got to give way over the secrecy,' Roger went on grimly. 'We've lost too much time already. Never mind what Shawn wants, never mind protecting him and his wife from hurt, stop wet-nursing them. I want Ricky Shawn's picture in every English newspaper in the morning. Every American paper, too – every newspaper in the world that will print it. If it's as vital as you say, then you want quick results, and secrecy won't get them, it will only slow us down. All I've been holding back from you and Lissa Meredith is that I don't like the hush-hush. It could kill your chance of finding that child quickly. You may throw away any chance of finding him at all.'

He talked quietly, standing by the desk, looking down on Marino; and Marino gave no indication of what he felt. It was some time before he spoke.

'I don't think it can be done,' he said.

'It's got to be done. Or I'll tell Hardy that I'm just wasting my time, and ask to be taken off the case,' Roger said. 'Look.' He took an envelope from his despatch-case, opened it, pushed a picture of Ricky Shawn in front of Marino, waited until the man had looked at it, drew out another. He held it out. 'Now look at this. That's Ed Scammel. That's what his throat looked like, after these people had finished with him.

They are the same people who hold Ricky Shawn. At the moment they've got us scared. Use enough publicity and they'll be the ones who are scared. When are you going to realize that?'

9

'REST' BY NIGHT

MARINO took the photograph of Scammel, placed it by the side of that of Ricky, and studied each closely without looking up. His big, pale hands did not move. Roger lit a cigarette, and blew smoke over Marino's head. The faces of Presidents looked down on him.

Marino glanced up.

'I will do what I can,' he said. 'I am not the big man.' He looked very bleak. 'Thank you, Roger. Even if they agree, it will take an hour or two. Call me in two hours, and I'll have the answer.'

'Do you mean that you're going to need Shawn's permission?' Roger demanded.

'I mean I'll do all I can.'

'If Shawn holds it up, let me handle him,' Roger said.

Marino chuckled, unexpectedly. Roger smiled and relaxed, accepted another drink, and asked without tension:

'Where is Lissa?'

'With David Shawn. Now that he's cooled down a bit, she can cope. He won't throw her out of any window. There are two or three of our men down there, you have no need to worry. We're trying to make sure that if Shawn gets a message, he won't keep it to himself. The most likely one he'll talk to is Lissa, so she will stay closer than a sister. Unless you need her for something else, that is.'

'I should hate to think she wasn't doing something useful,'

Roger said lightly. Gaining his point with Marino had given him brief but sweet satisfaction, and he didn't actually miss Lissa now. 'I won't call you about sending that photograph out, I'll have Bill Sloan do that. If you give the go-ahead, he can fix everything.'

'What are you going to do?'

'First I'm going home,' said Roger. 'I've a wife and family. Afterwards, I'm going to Clarice Norwood's house.'

'Why?'

'The lady's left it empty, and Gissing might be planning to use it. Obviously he might have wanted her out of the way in case we trace the Austin to the house, but why should we take that for granted? Ask me again, and I'll say I've got a hunch!'

'I told you,' Marino said. 'Lissa can pick men.' He tapped Scammel's photograph. 'Be very careful.' To emphasize the words, he took a small automatic from his pocket and held it out. 'I know you Yard men don't carry guns without special permission. I talked Hardy into agreeing that you should. Use this until you can collect yours from the Yard.'

Roger took it. 'I will,' he said. 'Thank you.'

The tapping of Marino's finger seemed like a warning of disaster; the little gesture, so deliberate and full of meaning, hovered in front of Roger's eyes as he went out into the welcome cool of the evening. The gun made an unfamiliar weight in his pocket. He drove to the Yard but did not trouble to collect another gun. He went to the canteen with Sloan, had supper and made plans, as carefully as if he knew that Gissing would go to the house. After eight-thirty, when dusk was falling, he turned into Bell Street, Chelsea, where he lived. He would only have a few minutes, for he wanted to be at 'Rest' by full darkness, but it would be better than nothing. The street looked friendly and pleasant in the fading light, and neighbours waved. He pulled up alongside the house, and walked up the path as Janet opened the front door.

'Darling! I didn't think you were going to make it!'

'No faith in me,' Roger said. 'That's the trouble.' As they went indoors, he raised his head and sniffed. 'No odours of frying. No noises of tape recorder or television. I deduce that my two sons are not at home.'

They turned into the front room, which was pleasant but just a little shabby, for most of the furniture had been here for over twenty years. But it had comfort and charm.

'Scoop's out at some exhibition, they're showing three of his African paintings,' Janet said. 'And Richard rang up – he's a chip off the old block, I'm afraid.'

'What's he done that I wouldn't do if I could help it?'

'Working overtime. He has to go out on location, or something, he sounded very excited.' Janet watched as Roger poured out a modest tot of whisky and splashed in a lot of soda, and he got the impression she was waiting for something.

'What are you going to have?' he asked, although she seldom joined him except on special occasions.

'Nothing,' she said.

He sipped and frowned.

'Then what —' he began, and suddenly he remembered. 'God! What a clod I am! What did you buy?'

Her face lit up.

She had bought a suit in a blue-brown check which obviously she loved, and which she was sure was a bargain; he hadn't seen her happier for a long time, and for a short while, as he watched her face, he forgot the Shawns, Ricky, Marino and even Lissa.

Twenty minutes later, in a very different mood, he left the car in a yard near 'Rest' and walked along the side of the garden, under the trees towards the back door. No light showed. Plain-clothes police, patrolling the road, had signalled that no one had gone in. It could be, probably would be, a complete waste of time.

He let himself in with a key made at Scotland Yard's workshop, modelled from the soap impression he had taken on his last visit to the house. Using only his flashlight he left the kitchen and looked into each room. Nothing had changed. There was a faded easy-chair in the hall, and at the far end, beneath the stairs, a cupboard used as a cloakroom, big enough for him to hide in. Even if the door were opened, he could squeeze back, out of sight. He sat in the chair and put a cigarette to his lips but didn't light it. At first he found himself thinking of Scoop painting, and wondering what Richard, so much more intent and industrious, had been doing during the day on his scripts. His thoughts veered to Janet, then to Lissa Meredith. He found himself comparing them, in looks, in manner, and suddenly wrenched his thoughts away, to the missing Ricky and the dead Scammel.

Suddenly he heard a car approaching. Nearer it came, and nearer. He stood up as it stopped outside the house.

• • •

Roger waited by the front door, heard footsteps and retreated to the cloak-cupboard. He was inside, with the door open a crack, when a key turned in the lock. He couldn't see who came in, but the footsteps were those of a man. He heard a faint cough; then the light went on by the front door, not bright enough to show anything here. As his eyes became accustomed to the crack of light, he saw a man of medium height, wearing a black Homburg hat and a raincoat of a darker shade than that worn by the man who had followed him at Hammersmith Underground that afternoon. He took off the hat and coat and Roger made ready to draw further back; but the man flung them on to the easy chair, threw his gloves after them and went into the drawing-room.

A pale-faced man of middle age; that fitted this man and Gissing. Roger didn't move, heard the other walking about, fancied there was the chink of glass on glass. After a pause there came the unexpected, a bang of wood on wood followed by the rippling of fingers lightly touching the piano keys, then a melody, a familiar tune – *I'm Gonna Wash That Man right out of my Hair*. Its gaiety came to life, played well, as if the man enjoyed playing for its own sake. He went into other hits from *South Pacific* without pausing; he didn't need music. It was so normal, so light-hearted, that it seemed to mock any suspicion.

The man began to sing lightly, voice and music filled the house. Tunes from *My Fair Lady, Guys and Dolls,* then further back – *Annie Get your Gun* and *Oklahoma,* all without a pause, as if the player had come here just to do this.

Where was the touch of the sinister?

The music stopped, and the silence seemed to hurt, to be false. Sounds of movement followed, the drawing-room door opened. Roger didn't close the cloakroom door, he just drew back. The man walked towards him, and he held his breath. He couldn't see what happened, but the door slammed, as if the man had pushed it as he passed. Darkness surrounded Roger. He waited a few seconds, then opened the door a crack, heard water running from a tap, and the man humming. He re-closed it but kept his ear to the keyhole. He knew when the man passed, gave him time to reach the drawing-room again, then opened it once more.

There could be deadly danger here, if the house held danger. Gissing – was it Gissing? – had noticed the door open once, would be suspicious if he saw it open again.

He had played enough to satisfy himself, apparently, and it was very quiet. A clock struck ten. The chimes were light and clear, a friendly sound. As the last faded, Roger heard something else; another car.

He pulled the door so that it was almost closed, and he could only just see out. The old pattern was repeated – the slamming of a car door followed by footsteps. This time there was a sharp ring at the door bell. The pianist appeared, didn't look towards the cloakroom, just opened the front door. He hid most of the newcomer, but wasn't tall enough to hide David Shawn's rugged face.

If the face were not enough, the gruff voice with its undertone of harshness supplied everything that was missing.

'Are you the man who called himself Jack?'

'Jack' – and it was 'Jack' Gissing, thought Roger.

'I am,' said Gissing. His voice was pleasant and urbane, could easily have been the voice of the man who had telephoned Shawn at Wavertree Road. 'David Shawn, I presume.' Laughter tinged with mockery lurked in the voice. 'You must have shaken off anyone sent by the Embassy to follow you, or I would have had a telephone message by now. So we can talk freely. Come in.'

Shawn came in; Gissing wasn't small, but he was dwarfed. He looked up at the big man, smilingly, suave, quite self-possessed, untroubled by Shawn's hugeness. He closed the door. Shawn, without hat or overcoat, wearing the same grey suit that he had worn the previous morning, unruly hair roughly combed, face still like a piece of chiselled stone, looked down on him.

Roger couldn't see Shawn's eyes, but guessed what they were like; hot coals.

'I haven't come to talk,' Shawn said. 'I've come for my son.'

'And you shall have your son, quite safe and unharmed,' Gissing said easily. 'You needn't be at all worried about him, Mr Shawn. But we needn't stay here.'

He turned and led the way into the drawing-room. Shawn hesitated, glowering at his back, and then followed. Roger slipped out of the cupboard, closed the door softly, stepped across to the wall and crept towards the drawing-room. He opened the dining-room door next to it as a quick way of retreat.

'I told you I didn't come to talk,' Shawn growled.

'I know, I know,' said Gissing, and the laughter still lurked, as if the giant amused him. Yet Shawn's eyes must tell their story, and Shawn could crush him; if Gissing knew anything about Shawn, he would know that he was in acute danger. Judging from his voice, he didn't give the possibility a thought. 'We won't waste words, Mr Shawn, but there are one or two details to be settled. What will you drink?'

Shawn said: 'Where's my son? If you don't come across, I'll break your neck. Where is he?'

Gissing actually laughed.

'If you break my neck, how are you going to find your son?' he asked. 'Be sensible, Mr Shawn. Sit down. Whisky? Rye? Bourbon? There's ice in the kitchen – just wait a moment, and I'll go and get it.'

He was not a dozen feet away from Roger, and coming nearer.

10

BARGAINING

ROGER backed into the dining-room, but there was no time to close the door properly. Any movement would catch Gissing's eye, he would look up involuntarily. He might not notice that the door was ajar if it were not moving. Roger saw his shadow, and dropped a hand to Marino's gun.

Shawn said: 'You stay right here.'

'Mr Shawn, don't —'

Gissing looked as if he had suddenly been turned into a puppet pulled by its strings into a whirligig. The shadow of his arms, legs and head made crazy movements, then vanished. There was a thud, next a moment of silence before Shawn said thickly:

'I'll break your neck *after* I've broken up the rest of you. Where's my son?'

There was another moment of silence. Roger moved forward into the hall, taking a greater chance, and stood so that he could just see into the room; the door was wide open. He saw Gissing's feet and legs, on the floor. Shawn stood with his back to the door, blocking the rest of the room from Roger's sight.

'You don't seem to understand,' Shawn said, and his voice seemed higher-pitched, as if he were fighting for words. 'I've come here for Ricky, and if I don't get him, I'll kill you.'

Lissa had said that he had been hovering between sanity and insanity for a long time. No sane man would talk like this; no sane father would take such a chance with the man whom he knew or thought he knew had kidnapped his son. It could be a big bluff, of course, but was Shawn in a mood to bluff? He didn't sound like it. He sounded as if he thought that he could come here and find Ricky, and take him away; and if he didn't, he would kill.

Gissing made no attempt to get up.

Into the silence, Shawn said thickly: 'And a *gun* won't stop me.'

So Gissing had drawn a gun. Roger couldn't see it, could only see that neither of the men moved.

'If it comes to killing,' the Englishman said, 'I'll start. Don't be a fool, Shawn. I can tell you where to find Ricky, and I promise you he's not hurt. I had a message about him two hours ago.'

'Where is he?'

'Back in the States.'

Shawn's breath hissed. 'Whereabouts in the States?'

'You needn't know where he's been, all you want is to make sure that he comes back. To you – not to England. It was a mistake to bring him over here, Shawn. It was a mistake to come here at all. Go back home and wait, and he will be sent to you. The only thing he won't have is – this.'

Roger wished he could see, but dared not go farther towards the room. Shawn was standing quite still. Gissing's legs moved, as if he were dragging himself along the carpet, farther from the giant. Then his feet disappeared, and a hand showed, palm upwards for a moment. The finger ends were covered with a thin adhesive tape; to guard against leaving fingerprints.

A scuffle of movement told of Gissing getting up.

'Catch,' he said.

Shawn's right hand moved, clutched in the air and closed round something which Gissing had thrown.

'That's his,' said Gissing. 'The gold identity tag his mother had made for him to wear round his neck. He was asleep when it was taken off, and he doesn't know it's missing. See the mark in the corner? Where it dropped the first day he had it and carried it round in his hand? Remember that?'

Shawn didn't speak; Roger pictured his chest heaving.

'And I tell you he is perfectly all right,' insisted Gissing. 'All you have to do is go home, and take his mother with you. Then Ricky will be sent to you. No one will get hurt, you and your wife will be happy again.'

'She's happy right now,' Shawn said. The words came out in slow succession.

Gissing laughed; and as the sound came Roger knew that it was a mistake. Shawn's shoulders heaved as he flung himself forward. It happened too swiftly for Roger to do a thing. He waited for the roar of the shot, and actually moved forward, gun in hand, in readiness for an attempt to stop Gissing shooting again.

No shot came. Almost in the same moment that Shawn staggered backwards, Roger side-stepped out of sight. He saw Shawn's head on the ground, near the door, and pressed further back, but didn't think that Gissing would come any nearer. Shawn was breathing like a man with asthma; his head vanished as he struggled to his feet.

'I don't want to kill you,' Gissing said evenly. 'But if you do that again, I will. Go and sit in that chair.'

There was silence.

'Go and sit down, you great hulking fool,' Gissing rapped out. 'Sit down!'

There was a sound of movement, and the creaking, as of the man's bulk being lowered into a chair. Roger moved again so that he could just see inside the room. He saw Shawn's legs and feet, and Gissing standing sideways to the door. Gissing wasn't likely to look round, he was watching Shawn as he would a maddened tiger.

'I've told you how to get the boy back. I've made it easy for you. I've got two tickets for you on a jet leaving London Airport early tomorrow morning. You're going on that 'plane, Shawn. If you don't —' He stopped.

Shawn didn't speak, but the question must have been in his eyes. It seemed to Roger that Gissing revelled in this, relished the moment when he could hurt, by the pause, by the threat not yet shaped with words.

Still Shawn didn't speak.

'If you don't,' Gissing said, 'I'll give you tickets for another 'plane, in four days' time. The boy's right ear will be in the same envelope.'

Roger heard a horrible retching sound, as if dredged up from the depths of Shawn's heart.

Gissing waited for seconds which seemed like minutes, then moved a little nearer his victim, still covering him with his gun. Roger was holding his breath, as if resisting the brutality in Gissing's threat and the inevitability of what would happen if Shawn did not obey. This had been planned to the last detail, and there could be no way out while Gissing remained free to give his orders.

Then Gissing said briskly, coldly: 'That's all you have to do, Shawn. Leave now, tell no one where you've been or what you're going to do. Take your wife to London Airport on time. Here are the tickets.' He drew an envelope from his pocket and tossed it on to Shawn's lap.

As Shawn took it, his right hand appeared for an instant.

Gissing waited again; he used silence to twist the knife in the wound, to make the hurt lasting, unforgettable. Roger hadn't seen him clearly, knew him more from the deceptive softness of his voice than from his appearance; and from what he had said and how he had said it. In his way Gissing was as much a giant as Shawn. Lacking the larger man's physical strength, his was the strength of the utterly unscrupulous. This man mattered in the way that evil mattered. He knew exactly what he wanted, rode roughshod over everything to get it. Shawn might believe that once he was back in the States all would be well. Not likely. Any man but Shawn, any man not screwed up until his nerves screamed at him, would know that after the first demand would come the second; after the second, the third.

For the first time, Roger felt sorry for Shawn.

Watching the two men, Roger's entire attention had gradually been riveted on what he was seeing, what he was hearing, moment by moment. All thought had been numbed – and thought was only just beginning to come back. What next? He could stop Gissing now; he could stop Shawn too. While they were unaware of his presence they would be easy victims. Ought he to stop Gissing? *After the first demand, the second.* There was no way of being sure that Gissing was the only man who mattered; that if Gissing were caught it would be easy to trace the boy. It might be harder. Gissing might lead to the boy; so Gissing could serve a purpose if he were free.

There was more. Behind the kidnapping and the need for finding the boy, there was the work that Shawn was doing.

Reason said that Gissing might be one of many; at least of several. So ought he to let Gissing go as a sprat to catch a mackerel which might not exist. He had plenty of time to leave the house, walk up the private road and give the waiting police a description of Gissing's car. From the moment a warning went out, radio would trail him to his journey's end. Gissing couldn't escape the net once it was drawn around him. And there were only a hundred yards or so between Roger and the first pull at the net. Police forces in Great Britain could be alerted in a matter of minutes. France, the Low Countries, Eire, Northern Ireland – they would all co-operate.

Roger could see Marino again, give him his report, and leave him to handle Shawn. That wasn't his business, Shawn didn't matter in his investigations except where he got in the way.

Gissing said at last: 'You'd better have that drink.'

Once again Roger backed into the dining-room. Footsteps fell soft on the thick carpet. Gissing passed the door but didn't appear to glance towards it. He was a yard or two away when warning shouted in Roger's ear like a strident voice. Gissing wouldn't leave Shawn alone, not now, not knowing what Shawn might do. Gissing must realize that the man wasn't really sane; only in an emergency would he leave him and getting ice for a drink wasn't an emergency. Roger backed further into the room, gun covering the door, left hand behind him, stretched out for the table.

He saw a swift-moving shadow; and the light went on.

Gissing, gun in one hand, the other hand on the light switch, stood in the doorway. In that split second, Roger saw the man vividly, recognized the pale face, the dark eyes, the narrow chin – described by the Cornish sergeant. In the same split second he squeezed the trigger, aiming at Gissing's gun. The flash and the roar of the shot were simultaneous; he expected answering flame from Gissing's gun, had time to know it didn't come but none to see whether Gissing fell.

A weight crashed on to the back of his head. Pain first and then blackness swallowed him.

• • •

Pain and blackness were the first things Roger knew on waking, pain at the back of his head, and blackness, as if his eyes had been smeared with corrosive. He didn't move, just lay where he was, not thinking of Gissing, of Shawn, of anyone; conscious only of the pain and the darkness. Neither eased, but gradually thoughts began to trickle into his mind; first a vague recollection of fear and danger and then of shooting, the fact that he had fired. Then he remembered Gissing, and that he had not seen Gissing shoot. It might have been a bullet that had hit him. No, the blow on the back of his head hadn't been a bullet. Someone had been in the dining-room; someone had got in, while he had been listening to Shawn and Gissing, must have crept within a foot of him, and then waited.

The pain still wasn't easing, but now it no longer obsessed him. He felt the carpet with his fingers; a carpet, not necessarily at 'Rest'. Rest! He felt his mouth go taut, as if he were grinning in spite of himself. He pressed against the floor and began to reason as well as to remember. He must get up cautiously, if his hands and legs were free. That meant turning to one side, putting some weight on one arm, levering himself up. He moved his arms and legs, teeth gritting together against the new waves of pain. At least he wasn't tied up. He eased slowly over on to his left side, put his right arm over, drew his right leg up. He knew he was taking a long time; knew, too, that if he tried to be too quick, he would collapse again and lose more precious minutes. He must get to a telephone.

He might be locked in the room —

One thing at a time.

He clenched his teeth again. He felt as if his head was raw, his neck torn. Jagged pain struck at him when he lowered his head, and he hadn't the strength to move it up again quickly.

Go slow. Go *slow.*

Right hand against the floor, right knee over the left leg, right knee on the floor. Over, gradually, take the strain on right hand and knee. They were clawing at his head, ugly, jagged, ripping claws. And his head and face burned with a strange heat. He was getting up, he mustn't fall back, once on his feet he would feel better.

Up – up – *up*!

He stood swaying. The waves of pain were like waves hurling themselves against a leaking boat, he couldn't resist them, had to heel over.

He didn't fall.

After a while he stood without swaying, his feet well apart. He didn't know where he was, what he was looking at, because of the darkness; and it was utter darkness. He stretched out his right hand, went forward slowly and was less conscious of the pain. His fingers touched a wall. He turned right, hand against the wall, and went forward a step at a time. He kicked against something, and felt cautiously; his fingers told him that some kind of cabinet was in his way. He felt round it, touched something light; a glass fell, tinkling as it broke on the carpet.

His right foot crushed glass into the carpet, and he heard it crunch.

He found the wall again, then touched a picture, felt it move and heard it scrape. It swung back and touched his hand. He explored beyond that and went on again, until he touched something else, smaller and shiny. He kept still for a moment, then felt it carefully with his fingertips, until he knew that he was touching an electric-light switch. He had only to press it down, and there would be light. He longed for and yet feared it, because of the way it would strike at his eyes. As he closed them, and pressed down, he felt a moment of panic, in case the light didn't come on.

It came.

It was bright enough to show pale red through his eyelids,

but not too fierce to hurt. He stood quite still, then gradually opened his eyes. It was a dim light, and still didn't hurt; not enough to make him close his eyes again.

This was the dining-room; he was still at 'Rest'.

But Shawn wasn't and Gissing wasn't; he could be sure of that.

Where was the telephone?

What was the *time*?

II

MAN WANTED

ROGER looked at his watch. It was twenty-five minutes past eleven. Shawn had arrived at ten o'clock, just as the clock had stopped chiming. Allow an hour, an hour more or less, for the time they had talked in the drawing-room. Gissing had at least twenty-five minutes' start on him, perhaps three-quarters of an hour.

What of the watching police?

If they had known the others had left, they would have been here by now, so Gissing, Shawn, and his unknown assailant, had slipped them.

Roger opened the door and stepped into the square hall, then looked back into the dining-room; there was no telephone there. There wasn't one in the hall. He put on the drawing-room light.

He gasped and jerked his head. Pain seared through it, rushed to his shoulders, his back, everywhere – the pain of movement following the shock.

Shawn was still here.

He lay back in the chair in which he had been sitting when Roger had seen his hand move for the tickets. He didn't move.

His mouth was open, and his lips were moving, no he wasn't dead. Roger gave a sound that was almost a whistle; not dead, when he had expected him to be dead. Why? He didn't try to answer. This wasn't the time to think, he had one thing to do – call the Yard. The telephone was in a corner of the drawing-room, he remembered it now; a corner behind the door, near the window. As he edged towards it, he kept looking at the huge figure slumped in the chair. The telephone was a long way off. Ten feet. Eight feet. Movement was more difficult now, his head didn't hurt so much, but it was swimming, and the room began to sway round him. He leaned against the wall, breathing hard, made himself stay there for some time before moving again.

Six feet. Four.

He lunged forward, grabbed the telephone, clutched it first time, and grinned, as if at an enemy he had fooled. Resting his shoulders against the wall, he raised the instrument to his ear, then put his right hand towards the dial. His finger seemed to be going round in circles. Must keep it steady. He dialled W, the first letter in Whitehall 1212, the most familiar number in his life, before he realized that there had been no dialling tone. He found a spurious energy, rattled the platform up and down, and tried again.

The telephone was dead.

'Ought to have known,' he said. The words sounded loud. 'Wire cut.' He looked at the instrument stupidly, closed his eyes, and fought another spasm of giddiness. When he opened them again he was looking straight at some bottles on a tray. Whisky – gin – soda. He wanted a drink, to pull himself together, nothing would do that like a drink, but – his head. Spirits would go straight to it, make the pain worse; it might knock him out. The bottles shone, straw-coloured, honey-coloured. The colour of *clear* honey. Where had he seen clear honey lately? Ah! Lissa's eyes.

The bottles leered like wanton demons. He turned his back

on them and on the figure of Shawn, but couldn't get rid of the mental picture of the man, mouth drooping open, face looking ugly. Then he realized why, at the first glance, he had thought Shawn to be dead. The man's eyes were hidden by their lids, and his life was in his eyes.

He must get outside, the cool air would do more good than whisky. It wasn't far along the road. What was a hundred yards? Three hundred feet. He was thinking with the deliberation of a drunk, and he wouldn't have even a sip of whisky. That proved how completely he was in control of himself. No whisky.

He opened his mouth.

'*Stop talking like an idiot!*'

The words seemed to echo at him from the wall, but they did him good. He went to the door cautiously, but without support, then turned towards the front door. Of course the crisp night air would revive him, and he could rest on his way to the main road and the watching police.

His hand was on the front-door latch when he heard the car approaching.

He kept his hand there for some seconds, fighting against this further shock, and telling himself how far he was from normal. Who was this? The police? Gissing? Or one of Gissing's men? Probably Gissing, so he must take precautions. The trouble was, he couldn't move swiftly. He backed slowly towards the treacherous sanctuary of the dining-room. It wasn't any use putting out the lights, whoever had come would have seen them by now. He stepped back into the dining-room, as he heard footsteps, but his back was against the light, he had no cover there. Then he realized that the cloakroom opposite was in darkness, offering a kind of safety. He went slowly across the hall towards it, as footsteps sounded on the porch. He listened with great care, head tilted to one side, and solemnly came to a conclusion which at first didn't surprise him.

A woman was approaching.

A woman? Why should a woman —

The bell rang and the knocker clanged; both sounds went agonizingly through his head. He felt in his pockets, foolishly; of course, he hadn't the gun. The bell kept ringing, the knocking continued furiously; and then both stopped and the footsteps started and faded. Was she going away? Would she give up so quickly? Who was she? Gissing's woman? Or Belle – Belle, after Shawn?

He heard a crash of glass in the drawing-room, and realized that the woman had gone to the window and smashed it. He heard glass falling for what seemed a long time afterwards. He looked around, saw a golf club standing in a corner. He moved for it, making himself go slowly; every jerk, every attempt at speed, sent the pains shooting through his head and neck. Club in hand, he went to the hall, heard more glass break and an explosive:

'Goddam that glass!'

Roger went in, no longer nervous, but not relieved, for Lissa was here.

How had she discovered the address?

• • •

Lissa's back was towards Roger as he entered the drawing-room. One leg was inside the window. Her skirt was drawn up above the stockings, showing bars of pink suspenders against the golden tan of her leg. She lowered her head carefully, brought head and shoulders into the room, then drew the other leg after her; before turning, she raised her right hand to her lips and began to suck. In spite of the awkward way she had come in, grace gave beauty to every movement. Roger stood and watched her, club in hand, and suddenly she swung round, surprised; frightened?

Her tension vanished.

'Roger!' She came towards him, arms outstretched. 'My

God! You look terrible. You mustn't stand there, sit down.'

As she took his elbow, blood welled up from a cut on the back of her right hand. Ignoring this, she guided him to an upright chair. She glanced at Shawn only once, and seemed to forget him. When Roger was sitting, his head thumping but the rawness of the pain at bay, she stood back and scanned his face; concern turned her eyes to a glowing golden colour.

'How – did you get here?'

'Don't move,' she said. 'Just sit still.' She went behind him, and he felt the touch of her fingers on his head; they hurt, and he flinched. He knew that she was parting the blood-matted hair, trying to see how badly his scalp was cut. After a few seconds her fingers seemed to soothe. Then she went on: 'I don't think it's too bad. I'm going to bathe it.' She turned away.

'Lissa! Come back, I want you to —'

'Be quiet, there's a honey,' she said, and was gone.

She came back with water in a bowl, a towel and a sponge.

'Now, I'll bathe your head, and afterwards —'

'Put those down!' he shouted at her. 'Go to the front door. Flash a light, five times. *Now*. Put those things down I tell you!'

She put them down, asked no question, took a pencil-slim torch from her handbag and went out again. She was soon back, went behind him, and very gently laid the wet sponge on his forehead.

'I'm all right,' he muttered. In fact, he felt tired now – only one thing kept his mind probing: the fact that she hadn't answered his question – how had she got here?

'Sure, you're wonderful,' she said. 'You could spend the whole night searching for Ricky.' She moved away but was still behind him, and he didn't want to turn his head. He heard a snap, perhaps of a handbag opening. Then she appeared in front of him, with two white tablets on the palm of her hand. 'Aspirins,' she said. 'I'll get you some fresh water.'

She fetched a glass from the tray, then put the tablets to his mouth one at a time, and gave him a sip of water after each. His teeth touched her palm as she tipped his head back gently and the tablets went into his mouth.

He was trying to explain away her arrival, to make out an easy, satisfactory case for it, although he was beginning to doubt the part she was playing.

She stood back, with the glass in her hand.

'Roger, you had me worried, and you still look terrible.' But she said that light-heartedly. 'You need a doctor this time.'

She was relieved about something, and it could hardly be about him. She couldn't have any real concern for him. Could she? He wished that he had his wits about him, that he could toss the urgent questions at her without making it clear that he had doubts.

'I'm all right.' He wanted to ask her again how she had discovered this address, but didn't.

Lissa moved across to Shawn. Beauty and the beast – yet the man had seemed comparatively handsome the previous morning. Dishevelled hair, black stubble, the big slack mouth and the closed eyes all detracted from his looks. Lissa, who had been bending over him, shrugged and turned away.

'I followed him, of course,' she said. 'I was to look after him, remember. He must have had a message before you tapped the telephone wire. There were three of us at the house tonight,' she went on, moving towards Roger. 'Let me help you up – that club chair will be more comfortable, you can stay there until a doctor comes. I'll telephone. One of the three had to stay, in case Belle had a visitor. Shawn discovered the other was following him, and he did his window trick again. Nearly! He didn't see me. There's been a nasty accident, at the corner – a man crushed to death. There was some trouble getting through, but David managed to pass. I had a bigger car. I didn't want an argument with your police, anyway, so I left the car and walked.'

She pulled him up, gently, although he could have managed by himself now. They began to walk across the room, and she slid an arm round him. He didn't need support but he didn't object.

'I saw David come down this road, but had to leave the car and walk from the corner. I was twenty minutes or so behind him, and wasn't sure this was the house – or that David was still here, even if it was. Then I heard voices, and recognized his. I went round the house to try to get in, but all the doors were locked, and I daren't break a window then. I didn't know how many people were inside. Now, easy, Roger. Pull on me.' His back was to the easy chair, and she gripped his hands; she was slender as a sapling, but strong enough to hold him steady as he lowered himself gently. The upholstered chair was much more comfortable. 'Now I'm going to ring for a doctor,' she said, 'and then I'm going to bathe your poor head again.'

'The telephone is out of order,' Roger croaked.

She didn't speak, but took the bowl of water, pink with blood, and went out.

She had told half the story, convincingly; in those swift, coherent sentences, interrupted only by orders to him. It had been told as the truth might be told, casually, without concentration, just between pauses when she wanted to do something else. If she could explain what she had done after that half-hour, he would be satisfied.

He heard her coming back.

12

OFF DUTY

SHE came towards Roger, carrying the bowl, and the sight of her did much to melt the ice of suspicion. She smiled, as if he were the only man to know her favour. Something in her look told him that she guessed what he was thinking, that it amused her, and she was ready to indulge him. In some curious way she made him feel that she regarded him as precious; hers.

'And then a man came out of the garage,' she went on, taking up the story as if she'd never broken off. 'He must have seen me prowling. He kicked a stone, or I wouldn't have known he was there. I turned and *ran*. He blundered after me, and we played hide-and-seek among the trees and the bushes over there.' He knew there was a patch of bushes, laurel, rhododendron and hawthorn, at one side of the garden. 'I didn't enjoy it,' she went on, and meant that she was terrified. 'It was like being stalked by a big cat. It's a lonely place, Roger. Then there was a shot from the house, and the man went rushing across to see what had happened. I caught my coat on some thorns.'

Yes, her coat had several tiny tears in it.

'It seemed hours before I got free,' she went on, 'and before I went to the house they drove off in a car. I saw two men, anyhow. David's car was there, with the ignition key still in it, so I got in and followed them.'

And he had suspected her!

'Did you —'

'The car was difficult to start, and that delayed me; I knew I couldn't catch up with them, so I drove back here. It's been quite a night, Roger.'

'Quite a night,' he echoed faintly. All this, and plain-clothes men had been nearby; they would hear plenty soon.

'I'm a fool,' Lissa said. 'You must be cold.' She hurried out of the room, and he heard her running up the stairs, walking overhead, then running down again. Her story didn't account for the man in the dining-room, but if there had been one outside there might well have been another, who could have got in and reached the dining-room, keeping quiet after Roger had moved from the cupboard under the stairs.

Lissa brought blankets, wrapped them round him, tucked them in, bathed his head once again; and all the time gave the impression that only he mattered.

'Now I'll make you some tea,' she said. 'Or would you prefer coffee?' From the door, she asked: 'What should happen, after I flashed that light?'

'Chief Inspector Sloan should soon be here.'

In fact, Sloan arrived as Roger was sipping hot, sweet coffee, and as Lissa was standing in front of a mantelpiece mirror, drawing a comb through her hair with slow, almost sensual movements. Sloan had two plain-clothes men with him. He had come across the river in a launch, held ready, and been prepared for trouble. Roger didn't like his expression; and one of the others looked as if he were suffering from shock. Roger didn't tie that up with the accident Lissa had mentioned.

He didn't know anything more about the accident until the doctor arrived, to examine his head wound. An incautious remark earned a scowl from Sloan, and told Roger something was badly wrong. Once he forced questions, Sloan didn't hold out. The two plain-clothes men who were 'soon going to hear plenty' had been patrolling the main road right and left from the private road, there simply to watch and report all comers. They met every fifteen minutes, to compare notes. They had been comparing notes when a car had run into them. One was dead, and with the other it was touch and go.

All of this was in keeping with the tempo of the crimes. Drugging, kidnapping, a slashed throat, now crushed and broken bodies. The car was a hired car, the driver had escaped. The 'accident' must have happened just after Shawn had arrived. No one was known to have seen Gissing and then Shawn come – except Roger. There seemed little doubt that Roger had been left for dead.

As he listened, with a thick towel round his neck while the doctor snipped blood-matted hair, Lissa was stand-in for a nurse.

'You'd better have a bandage,' the doctor said, 'You won't like it, but you need it. The cuts aren't too bad, I don't think anything's cracked. Might X-ray, to make sure. What you need is rest.'

'I can't *rest*.'

'You try getting about,' said the doctor ominously, 'and you'll go out on your feet.'

'I'll take you home,' Sloan offered.

No one asked the obvious question, which was stabbing into Roger's mind. They had killed Ed, crushed the watching police, yet they hadn't killed *him*. Why not? *Had* they left him for dead? One shot or one slash with a knife would have made certain, but they hadn't been ruthless with him.

He had to be helped to Sloan's car, and helped inside. His head seemed twice its usual size, and it kept lolling about. Sloan held one of his arms, Lissa the other. When he was in the car Lissa tucked blankets round him, and her touch comforted.

'Take care,' she said. 'Do what they tell you, Roger. Goodnight.'

'Goodnight,' Roger replied.

Sloan moved off, cautiously, and they were past the scene of the accident and on the way to Hammersmith Broadway before he spoke. Then it was almost to himself, wonderingly; and it wasn't about the slaughter.

'Some woman,' he said.

Roger didn't answer.

• • •

Whether he liked it or not, Roger knew he would be off duty for forty-eight hours, and it might be much longer. He was hazy about what happened after he reached Bell Street. Janet had been warned, everything was ready, Sloan helped her to undress him and get him to bed, the doctor looked in and gave him a shot which blacked everything out. He was only vaguely aware of Janet's ministrations, of light and movement, and he couldn't think clearly, although he knew that there was plenty he ought to think about. He was cut off from the case of a missing child and tormented, half-demented parents, and that all-compelling reason for secrecy.

He hadn't even asked Sloan or anyone else whether Marino had agreed to giving a hand-out to the Press.

• • •

Roger slept until after midday. When he awoke he felt much better, his head now shrunk to proper size, and only a threat of pain when he moved it, or when he ate and drank. Janet knew there was no hope of keeping the newspapers from him, and had bought all the dailies. In each there was a picture of Ricky Shawn, and a story which told the world this was kidnapping for money. There was a picture of Belle Shawn, too, a laughing picture of a lovely woman. There was none of Shawn. The papers told Roger nothing, except that he'd had his way. Reading, he was teased by an uneasy thought, that he had forgotten something significant – something he'd heard which could be a key to the puzzle.

Marino telephoned to inquire after him, so did Hardy. He expected a message from Lissa, but it didn't come. Sloan looked in, told him that Shawn had been taken away from 'Rest' by two men who arrived from the Embassy; Sloan didn't know what had happened to Shawn. The blanket of official secrets fell like a dead hand on the case. Roger felt irritated and glum, and put it down to the obvious – that the Yard had been consulted but wasn't being allowed to work properly. The Yard should have tackled Shawn. The Special Branch or even MI5 might be working on the case with the Americans, of course – but if so, why had the Yard been consulted in the first place?

With time to think without the pressure of events chasing him, Roger thought he understood. In the early stages the Yard had been needed, to deal with the local police, neighbours, everything. If he hadn't been injured he would probably still be working on it, but by the time he was able to get about again, the case might be over.

That forgotten factor still teased him.

Now and again, resting and even dozing, his body would grow tense. An image of Gissing's face in the doorway of the dining-room would come, showing all the evil and the deadliness. As Lissa was beauty, so was Gissing ugliness; corruption. It was thinking extravagantly, but he couldn't rid himself of the thought. Gissing – corruption. In the moment of revelation the man had been stripped of the veneer covering his unholy, deadly self.

In the evening, the boys came home, commiserated, and went off, Scoop to his exhibition, Richard to see a film.

The next day passed, and Roger learned nothing more. Lissa had not inquired. There was nothing new from the newspapers, from Sloan or from Marino, who telephoned again. This time, Roger spoke to him from the bedroom extension, wanted to ask questions, to prompt Marino to talk about the case, about Lissa; but Marino would talk of neither, just told him not to worry and hoped he would soon be on his feet.

'Tomorrow,' Roger said grimly.

'You stay in bed,' Marino advised.

Roger put down the receiver, stared at the ceiling and felt as if there were a conspiracy against him. It probably meant the end of the case for him, and if it hadn't been for that bloody blow over the head, he would have been in it up to his neck. Finding Ricky Shawn was his job; and finding the man who had run down the police officers was also his. He mightn't be able to do it – oh, to hell with it all! He picked up a newspaper and began to skim through the headlines, then to read '*American Letter*' in the *Telegraph*. He was half-way through a hotch potch of political guesses when there was a rat-tat at the front door.

Martin, who was in for once, went to open it.

'A cable,' he said, marvelling. He came striding up the stairs and burst into Roger's room, calling: 'A cablegram, Dad – *Western Union*.'

Roger slit it open eagerly, heard Janet coming upstairs, wondered without trying to think deeply, and read:

> 'Get well soon sorry I had to leave without
> seeing you Lissa Meredith'

The cable was from New York.

Roger stared at it, and the name especially. He didn't realize that Martin was looking at him in bewilderment, or that Janet had come in. When he did wake up to that and look round, Janet was watching him with a strange intentness, and in an unfamiliar, even voice she said:

'Put a kettle on, Scoop, will you?' When the boy had gone, with obvious reluctance, she closed the door. 'What is it, darling?' she asked.

She spoke as if she knew that it was bad news, and Roger realized in that moment that he looked as if it were deadly. He realized, too, that this was because Lissa Meredith was in New York, three thousand miles away. He had to find an explanation for Janet, to stop her from springing to the obvious conclusion. He flung the cable aside, and growled:

'From New York. Mrs Meredith's gone back, everything's been transferred there. It means the case is over, as far as I'm concerned, and I wanted to see the end of it.'

Tension faded from Janet's face. 'Oh, that's too bad,' she said, but couldn't hide her relief. 'Don't worry about it, darling.' She picked up the cable and read it; and obviously she hadn't the faintest thought that the name 'Lissa' had stabbed him savagely.

13

SPECIAL REQUEST

JANET said: 'You're sure you're all right?' and Roger laughed as he squeezed her arm and then walked to the car, which she had taken out of the garage. He wore a heavy top-coat and a light-weight felt hat, which hid the plaster on the back of his head and the patches where the hair had been cut away. It was a week since he had been attacked at 'Rest'. Except for tenderness round the patch, he felt quite normal as he waved to Janet, and drove off. The first dew of the autumn had been heavy, it still glistened white on the roof-tops, on the trimmed privet-hedges, and, where the sun hadn't reached it, on the pavement. The morning was fresh and invigorating, a good one to start work again.

In fact, he had been working at home.

Papers had been sent to the house, mostly about Yard business, keeping him up to date with cases under way when he had been taken off for the Embassy affair. He had skimmed them, as routine. The report from Hardy about the Shawn case had not been routine. He had read it several times, and knew it almost word for word. The airways tickets which the man he had thought was Gissing had given to Shawn had been bought from an agency, and the buyer had not been traced. The only cause for satisfaction was that Marino had asked that a copy of the report be sent to Roger.

The Shawns were back in their Connecticut home, fifty miles out of New York. Ricky Shawn had not been returned to them, although they had flown with Gissing's tickets. These were the cold facts of the situation, but Roger could read between the lines, and guess that Marino and others had tried to dissuade Shawn from returning to America but had decided to use no compulsion. Did it matter as much as Marino had said?

Would Marino have exaggerated?

Only Lissa Meredith had gone from the Embassy with the Shawns; and she was still with them, officially Shawn's secretary, actually to keep close watch on him, of course. It was hardly a woman's job, but there would be men at hand, Marino wouldn't be careless. There was no clear indication about the real part which Lissa played, except that she was Shawn's shadow.

There was the detailed report on the Yard investigation, which showed little in the way of results. The driver of the killer car hadn't been traced, and this was somehow worse because the second plain-clothes man had died. Soon afterwards, Shawn had admitted being told by telephone, before his line had been tapped, when to go to the house at Barnes. Sloan had theorized that Shawn had been followed by one of Gissing's men who had realized that Yard officers were near by and acted swiftly and ruthlessly. There was evidence that Ed Scammel had been thrown into the river from a jetty near Barnes Bridge, some distance from 'Rest'. The man named Jaybird had not been found, although he was now known to have been an associate of Scammel; he might be the man in the raincoat, might also be the killer driver.

The closely packed factual account made dry reading, as Roger searched in vain for anything to give an indication of Gissing's present whereabouts; and those of the missing boy.

Mrs Clarice Norwood was still in Paris. She had been interrogated by a Yard man sent to see her, but all she had said was that Gissing had sent her to Paris, for a 'holiday'. Gissing kept her, and the house was his under a covenant. She was worth watching, but it was by no means certain that she knew anything of Gissing's criminal activities.

There were a number of trifles, among them, that Ed Scammel had had a car of his own, an old Vauxhall, which he had kept in a lock-up garage, and which had been found with a broken axle.

Roger got out of his car at the Yard, waved and smiled mechanically to the dozen men of the uniformed branch who greeted him; maintained a chorus of 'Fine, thank you's' to those who asked him how he was, reached his own office and rang for Sloan, who came at once, obviously glad to see Roger back. He was massive and clean-cut, with a deceptive cloak of cherubic innocence that fooled a lot of people.

'You're seeing Hardy at eleven, aren't you?'

'Yes,' said Roger. 'I don't know what he wants, probably to tell me I'm lucky I'm not under the turf.' It was a quarter to eleven. 'Bill, that car of Scammel's.'

Sloan said: 'You beat me, you really do. You've seen what it means, I suppose.'

'I've wondered about it. What's the story?'

'The axle was all right on the morning of the kidnapping,' Sloan said. 'I mean, the morning before. Scammel went out from his lodgings in the early evening, came back, and was heard telephoning someone, saying that he couldn't use his car. It's pretty clear that the Austin was used because of that, isn't it?'

'It looks like it. Their one slip – Scammel's car couldn't have been picked up so easily as a new one. They used two, of course, the Austin at Ealing and the Buick at the airport – they didn't risk using the same car at both places. Anything else?'

'I was able to check with Mrs Meredith – my, what a woman!' Sloan was almost shrill. 'The only thing all three Shawns drank or ate that night was the milk. Except for that, the boy had different food altogether. His cup and everything he used had been washed up earlier. Everything you brought away was tested, and no drug found. The only luck we had was with the car.'

'Luck?' growled Roger. 'It didn't get us far. Any idea where Gissing is?'

Sloan didn't know, but was ready to guess.

'If you ask me, he's put a few thousand miles between himself and England. It's nearly eleven, you'd better not keep the old man waiting.'

Hardy was in his office, which was plain and nondescript, a little like Hardy, who had come up from the ranks and somehow gave an impression, at times, of being insecure because of it. A big man, usually dressed in clerical grey, now looking ill at ease in a black coat that didn't quite meet at the waist and striped trousers that were hoisted a few inches too high. He had a sallow face, grey hair with a bald spot, and lines at his pale grey eyes.

The morning dress meant an occasion.

'Just on time,' he said. 'I was going to send a warrant for you. We're due to see Marino.' He took his hat off a steel hat-stand, and looked Roger up and down. 'You seem all right. Been swinging the lead?'

The trouble with Hardy was that although he meant that as a joke, he sounded as if he were serious.

'It's one way to get a day or two off,' Roger said.

Hardy led the way to the lift, and was saluted by everyone they passed beneath the rank of Detective Inspector. His big black car was parked outside, and his chauffeur was at the ready. When they had settled in and the car moved off, Hardy asked: 'Seen the report on the Shawn case?'

'Yes, and I've talked to Sloan.'

'Then you know as much as I do,' said Hardy. 'If you ask me, Shawn would be easy to handle if it weren't for his wife.'

'Wives like seeing husbands occasionally,' Roger said slyly.

Hardy decided not to bite.

'The thing Marino worried about most was the possibility that the case has an espionage angle – that the aim of the kidnappers might be to stop Shawn working. Think there's anything in that?'

'I haven't a clue, and Marino admitted that he hadn't.'

'No one has, it just has the smell of it,' Hardy said. 'Another thing came in this morning, and Marino called me about it.'

Roger knew that this wasn't a cue for questions.

'You've got yourself in a fix,' Hardy went on. 'You seem to be the only reliable witness.'

'Of what?'

'Of Gissing's face,' Hardy answered, and shot Roger a sidelong look. 'Shawn won't or can't describe him, won't or can't try to identify him.'

Roger felt a sudden swift beat of excitement, and he damped down a wild hope.

'There is this Clarice Norwood woman, but we can't call her reliable,' Hardy went on. 'Notice from the report how few people seem to have seen Gissing? Everyone gives a different description. People have glimpsed him going to and from that riverside place of his, but only snatches of him, in the car. And one of our sergeants saw him during that Paris inquiry, but that's all. I hope your memory's good.'

'Where Gissing's concerned, it's photographic,' Roger said softly. 'What does Marino want?'

'Don't ask me,' said Hardy bluffly.

But he knew, and it wasn't simply that Marino wanted a

detailed description of Gissing.

'Is Gissing still in the country?' Roger made himself ask.

'If he were he'd be behind bars. Or I'd sack half the staff.'

They turned into Grosvenor Square, and in spite of heavy clouds blowing up, the usual photographers were shooting at the Roosevelt statue. The huge American cars, dwarfing all but a few Rolls-Royces and Hardy's black Daimler, seemed to gather for shelter beneath the waving flag of the Stars and Stripes.

Hardy had obviously been here before, he was recognized and taken in hand, and they were whisked up to Marino's office, where Herb, forewarned by telephone, was opening the door for them. He looked absurdly young.

'Come in, gentlemen, Mr Marino's free right now.' He opened Marino's door.

Marino didn't get up, even for the Assistant Commissioner of Scotland Yard. He stretched out his right hand, gripped Roger's firmly, searched his face and seemed relieved by what he saw. They sat down beneath the portraits of the august dead.

'I would offer you a drink,' Marino said, 'but I guess you'll say it's too early.'

'Think it's too early, West?' Hardy asked.

'Not if I'm off duty!'

Hardy grinned, Marino pressed a bell, Herb came in and produced an assortment of bottles. Marino poured out, making a formality of asking Hardy what it would be before he poured a whisky and soda. Herb went away.

'Well, now,' said Marino, 'you're very good to come over at such short notice, Mr Hardy. I surely appreciate that. You've been a great help from the beginning. I'm hoping you will be able to help even more.' Roger was glad of the drink, to help him cover his rising excitement. 'The way it's turned out, you're almost the only man we know who could recognize Gissing, Roger. And we want Gissing very badly.' He sipped his drink. 'And we think he's in the United States.'

'So that lets us out,' Roger said.

Marino's smile showed amiable disagreement. He leaned forward, with one of his rare body movements.

'And we think we can put a finger on him.'

Roger sat up, abruptly. '*Think*?'

'We can't be sure, because we haven't a photograph, finger-prints or anything else to go by,' Marino said. 'And we want him identified so that there can't be any doubt. We can't pick the suspect up until we've identification – unless he tries to take another powder, we would hold him then. I'm told you're often assigned to cases overseas, and in this case we certainly need your help, and you want Gissing as much as we do. Can you spare the Superintendent for a week or so, Assistant Commissioner?'

14

SUSPECT

EXCEPT for the perpetual drone of the four jet engines and an occasional lurch when the aircraft dropped through space and then went on as if nothing had happened, Roger would not have known that he was flying. By day, they had looked down fifty thousand feet or so to the Atlantic Ocean, which seemed flat and hardly ruffled. Occasionally they had sighted a ship. England was already three thousand miles away, and New York lay half an hour's flying time ahead. It was dark in the clouded heavens.

Roger had an empty seat beside him; there were several others in the cabin. Most of the passengers were dozing. Two, who had been air-sick after the first few minutes, were looking wretchedly in front of them. One of the two stewardesses walked from the little kitchen aft, smiled at Roger and disappeared into the crew's domain. A man snored faintly, a newspaper rustled.

In Roger's mind was a mixture of looking forward and looking back, and looking back was easier.

Looking back to Janet's startled exclamation when he had told her, her quick flash of 'Not again!' and then her quick 'I mustn't be silly, I'm sorry, darling', and her bright cheerfulness from then on until he had been ready to go. It was only the previous morning that Marino had said what he wanted.

The stewardess came out, and stopped by Roger.

'Won't be long now, Mr West, you'll see better if you move back, the wing is in your way here. There's an empty seat.'

'Oh, fine. Thanks.' He moved at once.

'It's wonderful by night,' the girl said.

'Wonderful' was just a word. The lights became brighter, a cloak of diamonds catching the eye and holding it. Flaming rubies and winking emeralds from the neon lighting as they drew nearer, the glitter from the windows of the skyscrapers which lit the sky, dark patches of the East and the Hudson Rivers, the floodlit funnels of the big ships and little ships lying alongside the miles of docks, a fantasy of light and dark, colour and shadow. They seemed unending, as if a moment in time had been caught and held, but the aircraft was losing height, belts were fastened – and then suddenly they were down, taxi-ing along the runway, and the tension which most passengers felt melted in relief. Everyone began to move and talk at once, the stewardesses called out: 'Keep your belts fastened for a minute, please.'

He had travelled as Mr Roger West, and hoped that no one knew him as an official from Scotland Yard. He was to be met privately at the airport and taken to the Milton Hotel. Marino had arranged everything.

The stewardess who had fussed him while on board shook hands, there was no trouble at Customs, just the unfamiliar accent and a different manner. A porter carried his two suitcases, he carried his briefcase, which had faked business papers – he had become a salesman for British-made cars. He could talk intelligently about cars. He scanned the little crowd waiting in the big, low-ceilinged airport terminal, and a young-looking man in a well-cut suit with broad shoulders, wearing a narrow-brimmed trilby, came up to him.

'Mr West?'

'Yes.'

'It's good to see you, Mr West. I'm Ed Pullinger of the FBI. I'm told I have to apologize for being Ed.' He had an open smile and an easy manner, his accent seemed strong to Roger, and he spoke more slowly than most men at home. 'I hope you had a good flight.'

'First-class,' said Roger.

'I'm very glad to hear it.' Ed led the way, and the porter followed. Outside, lights glistened on a vast mass of cars across the tarmac road; one car was drawn up by the exit. 'This is my car,' said Ed Pullinger, waving his hand towards a low-slung, gleaming giant of a Chrysler. 'Put those grips in the back,' he said to the porter, and tipped the man. 'Why don't you get in, Mr West.'

Roger started to get in, banged against the wheel.

'We drive on the wrong side,' Pullinger said. 'I should have warned you.'

Roger laughed and sat in pillowed comfort as Pullinger drove off. The car moved smoothly on its automatic gears. They swept along a nearly deserted road.

'The parkway,' Pullinger said. Traffic was all one way, and travelled fast – fast compared with London city traffic. 'We go over the Queensborough Bridge,' he continued. 'If it's your first visit, that's as good a way as any. Have you been here before?'

'Once – five years ago.'

'You've plenty new to see,' said Pullinger. He turned off,

and they followed a twisting road for a mile or so, then turned again into a road which was divided into three – two carriageways with a wide gap between. Soon, they were going through a brightly lit section; advertisement signs which dwarfed London's had a novelty which fascinated. They blinked, flashed, changed colour; they never stopped moving. 'This is Queens,' Pullinger said. 'Wait until you get to the bridge. Does Tony Marino still use his wheelchair?'

Roger's head jerked round.

'*What?*'

'Didn't you know?' Pullinger looked surprised, almost guilty. 'He's sensitive about it, I guess, although you wouldn't know it. He lost both legs during the war. Had a special wheelchair made. When he was here he used to sit at his desk and never move, looking at him you wouldn't guess.'

'I didn't realize why he never got up,' Roger said heavily.

Pullinger laughed.

'That would give Tony a big kick. A great guy, Tony Marino. Remind me to show you the letter I've got from him.' They were moving quickly past what seemed to be an endless stream of green lights at every intersection; the lights stretched out a long way ahead. 'Now we won't be long,' Pullinger said.

They reached the long approach to the Queensborough Bridge, with its cobbled surface; turned corners; and were suddenly on the bridge itself, tyres humming oddly on the metalled surface. Ahead, the lights of the skyline stood out against the pitch-black sky. From above, they had seemed brilliant; here they scintillated. They didn't seem real.

Pullinger kept up a running commentary.

'The one with the red vertical line at the top is the Empire State Building, that top part's used for television transmitting. There's the Chrysler Building.' They were jewelled swords, blades pointing skywards; thousands of windows and thousands of bright lights. 'It's some city,' Pullinger said. 'It's the finest city in the world.' He glanced sideways, expecting a challenge.

'I'll argue when I get to know it better,' said Roger. 'Just now, I'm trying to remember everything.'

He found himself thinking of the reason for Marino sitting in the same place and seldom moving his body. Nothing else about the man had suggested he had been so crippled.

'Fifty-seventh Street,' said Pullinger. 'One for shops.' He named the avenues they passed. The lights seemed brighter than in Queens, traffic was thick, huge yellow, red and blue taxis crowded the streets. 'Broadway,' said Pullinger. 'I'll drive you to Times Square, and then you can go and recover at your hotel. You don't have to work tonight.' He turned left, there was no change in the street scene until they turned a bend in the road, and ahead of them light seemed to blaze from the ground and from the sky. 'More lights in that square mile than any other place in the world,' said Pullinger.

'It looks it,' Roger said faintly. He laughed. 'And it's real.'

'You'll learn how real. The Milton's on 44th Street, only a step from Times Square, Tony said to put you in the heart of things. Say, Mr West, would you like to have dinner with me? The hotel food is pretty good, I guess, but if you're not too tired, we could go down to the Village, or any place you like.

'The Village sounds fine! I'll wash and freshen up.'

'I'll see you to your room and then leave you for an hour,' said Pullinger. 'Give you time to get an appetite. You'll need one.' He had all the brightness and frankness of Herb, Dr Fischer, and the others at the Embassy. 'It's not a big hotel, but it's good.'

The Milton Hotel had an unexpectedly old-fashioned look, and the foyer was half empty. Roger signed a slip of paper, not a book; a bell-hop, looking too small for the two big suit-cases, took them up to the ninth floor; Room 901. Pullinger ordered drinks, right away. The room was on a corner, with windows in two walls. Lights flashed on and off from nearby signs; a police siren shrilled out down below, a car blared and went on blaring.

'Don't let me forget that letter,' Pullinger said, and took out a billfold not unlike Ed Scammel's but made of alligator skin. He handed Roger a letter. It was on the Embassy note-paper, signed by Marino, and ran:

'Dear Roger,

Ed Pullinger, the bearer of this letter, will do right by you. Tell me if he doesn't. Don't exhaust yourself looking at Gissing, there will be plenty to see.'

The drinks arrived, Roger's a straight whisky and soda, Pullinger's a small glass of Bourbon and a tall glass with three ice cubes in it. He poured the Bourbon, and Roger watched it cascade down the ice cubes.

'How much do you know about the Shawns?' Roger asked.

Pullinger shrugged.

'I'm David's cloak and dagger when he's on this side. I was around when he was shot at in his Connecticut house. If you believe him, I pushed him away from an auto that was going to run him down. You might say that Shawn built up my reputation for me!' Pullinger offered cigarettes from a golden coloured packet.

'Thanks.' Roger took one.

Pullinger went to the door. 'I'll call you when I'm back, but it won't be for an hour. See you.'

He went out, and Roger drew on the cigarette and then went to the window and looked down on to the sea of dancing light, heard the din of traffic, even the footsteps of the crowds on the pavement. He laughed at himself, opened one case, took out a clean shirt, his shaving-gear, everything he would need. When he was in the middle of shaving in a bathroom which had everything, including a tap marked 'Iced Water' – and it was ice cold – he yawned.

He hadn't slept much on the journey or the night before. He might have been wiser to have a walk round the streets by himself and come back to his room early. He couldn't disappoint Pullinger now – 'Ed' wanted to show off a New York he obviously loved. And why not? Roger yawned again. He finished shaving. He had half an hour to spare, and ten minutes in a comfortable-looking armchair wouldn't do any harm. It would be pleasant to close his eyes.

He went to sleep.

He was still asleep, nearly an hour later, when the door opened and two men came in. One was stocky, with broad shoulders and a swinging walk. He had a wide-brimmed hat, and was smoking a cigar. He didn't smile. The other did smile; stepping across to Roger, he looked down, and said lightly:

'He'll have a shock when he comes round.'

'Who said he was coming round?'

'I did. We have to get him away, we don't have to leave a body. You're going to help me dress him. Then we'll take him down between us. Just another drunk. Gene will have the car outside, all ready for him.'

'Where are you going to take him?'

'Someone forgot to tell you not to ask questions.'

'Who is the guy?' the stocky man said, but didn't expect an answer. He looked at a BOAC label on a suitcase. 'British, eh? You can tell he's a foreigner.' He went round to the back of Roger's chair, and Roger didn't stir. 'Jesse! Take a look at the back of his head.'

'I heard about that,' said the other. 'Take a look at his coat and get him into it.'

That didn't take long.

They poured whisky into a glass, splashed a little into Roger's face, over his coat and shirt, then rumpled his hair, pulled his tie to one side, unfastened his collar. Then the man with the big shoulders pulled Roger to his feet, put one of

Roger's arms round his neck, and dragged him towards the door. They got him to the elevator, his feet scuffing the carpet. The elevator man didn't blink an eye.

No one in the hall took much notice. A woman stared disgustedly, and turned her back. A car drew up at the kerb as they appeared outside the hotel, which was poorly lit compared with most of the shops and buildings. It was a big Dodge, black, several years old. They bundled Roger into it. His head lolled back, he sat slumped into the corner, with one man by his side. The broad-shouldered man didn't get in. The driver, who didn't speak, slid into the stream of traffic. They turned right and right again, then drove straight out to the Hudson River Parkway, got on to the parkway at 57th Street, then drove fast towards the toll stations and on towards the Merritt Parkway and Connecticut.

Roger still slept.

The lights of New York lit up the sky behind him.

15

LIGHT

ROGER had a sense of having slept for several hours; a sense of vanished time; a void he couldn't fill but which he knew had been peopled with men and swift movement. It was dark, but this time he had no pain, only a numbness in his head and limbs and heaviness at the back of his eyes. He felt no sense of alarm, and he was quite comfortable. He began to try to remember, and at first it seemed that there was something in the past which was all-important, but he couldn't recall what it was. Then pictures flashed on to the retina of his mind – Marino and all that had followed, a thin-faced child, Lissa, the airport, Janet, the boys, the flight, New

York and a smiling, loose-limbed youngster who seemed to be one of a pattern stamped out and freely used at Grosvenor Square. With all this, a feeling persisted that some vital factor had been presented to him, but he couldn't place it.

Ed Pullinger, a promise of dinner in Greenwich Village, a wash and shave and the easy chair.

He wasn't sitting, now, he was lying at full length, and he knew that he hadn't just come round after forty winks.

The numbness discouraged him from trying to move, but he threw that off and sat up. It was no effort and brought no pain. His feet touched the floor, and the couch or bed gave beneath him. He stood up. The darkness remained, thick and impenetrable, but it didn't blanket sound. He heard a man's footsteps, sat down again, dropped back and lay in the position he had been in when he had come round. The footsteps drew nearer, heavy and deliberate; he heard another sound, which might have been the jingling of keys. Tension gripped him. The man stopped, there was a moment's pause – and then a shaft of light streamed into the room.

It missed his eyes, yet still dazzled him. It came from a square hole on the other side of the room, not far away. Then a shadow darkened the light, and he made out the shape of a man's head; another light came on, inside the room, bright enough but not dazzling. The shadow faded and the other light went out, as if it had been cut off, then the room light was doused. The footsteps receded, until only the brooding silence kept him company.

He had been hypnotized by the light from the square hole, had stared that way, without looking about him, but now the picture of the room formed slowly in his mind. He was in a corner, with his head near a wall. There were two armchairs, an upright chair and a small table – he could place them within inches. In the far corner was a hand-basin; he even remembered a glass standing on the shield above the basin.

He stood up cautiously and moved about, testing his mind-pictures and finding them correct. The room was no more than ten feet square, there was nothing on the walls, nothing he had noticed. He reached the door, and felt it with the palms of his hands, until he touched the edge of the square window through which the first light had come. He traced the outline of this window with his fingers, then spanned the side of the square between his thumb and little finger. It was about fifteen inches, base and side. He drew back, forcing all his thoughts on to it. There was a hole cut in the door; on the other side a panel had been removed or swung back, admitting light from the room or passage beyond. That light was probably still on.

He turned away.

The room was uncomfortably warm, and he hadn't realized that before – he had generated his own heat out of the tension. He felt dry, and groped his way to the hand-basin, feeling cautiously for the glass, then for a tap. He didn't know whether it was hot or cold. He ran it for a few seconds, and it kept cold, so he pushed the glass under it. Water spilled over his hand and splashed on to his coat. He had a drink, but not too much, waited, then drank again. That was much better. He turned back, heading for one of the easy chairs, his hands stretched out because he hadn't all his bearings yet. He touched it – and a light split the darkness, swift and blinding, then went out.

He snatched his hand away from the chair.

The darkness seemed worse now.

Had the light come on when he had touched the chair – or had it been coincidence? He tried again. Nothing happened. He sat down and tried to relax, but that blinding light had left him more uneasy and disturbed. He waited for it to come again, but nothing happened. For a few minutes he couldn't bring himself to think clearly, but gradually the effect of the light faded.

What had happened after he had sat down for a nap?

He hardly needed to think. He had been drugged and brought away from the hotel, but he needed to exercise logic as a child repeated the ABC. He had been drugged. Someone had drugged him. Who?

Ed Pullinger?

He had smoked one of Pullinger's cigarettes; and they had both had a drink sent up to them. His a whisky and soda, Pullinger's a Bourbon on the rocks. Roger had watched the Bourbon pour out of the little glass and cascade down the three small lumps of ice in the long glass, just like Marino's way of drinking. The dope might have been in the cigarette, then, or it might have been in the drink. Pullinger might have been doped, too.

He must keep a clear mind.

He laughed, and that didn't do him any good. How would a clear mind help him? Where was he? Who —

Light flashed!

It seemed to scorch his eyes with white heat, was as blinding as the darkness, he sat with his hands clenched, every nerve taut. A swift succession of flashes, each as vicious as the last, went on and off, as if it would never stop; but it did stop.

He didn't relax. Sweat fell slowly down his forehead to his cheeks. He was wet with sweat; lips, neck, cheeks and the darkness gave him no rest. It was a long time before he settled back in his chair, and began to turn his head. He wasn't sure where the light had come from – in front, above or behind him. It wasn't here now, but it seemed to be, his eyes were alternately blinded with the glare and with blackness. Gradually, blackness won.

This was deliberate, of course, part of the process of breaking him down, but he didn't know why he was being broken down. He felt in his pockets again, as if cigarettes and matches might have come back miraculously, but each pocket was empty. He stood up and began to move about, his clothes sticking to him. The darkness remained, so black that it was hard to believe that anything could break it. Slowly, his nerves settled down, not to normal, but at least free from hurtful tension. He touched each chair, the table, the bed and the hand-basin, had another drink of water, and was putting the glass down when the searing light flashed again.

He dropped the glass, and heard it smash.

He gripped the side of the hand-basin so tightly that his fingers hurt.

The light went on, off, on, off, striking viciously each time, but after the first few seconds he felt steadier, was able to think consciously of fighting against the breaking-down process. This was only light, it offered no danger, was no threat in itself. It would stop in a few minutes, and darkness would come again, giving him rest. He waited for the flashing to stop, much longer than before. It stopped at last, but not in the same way. The light stayed on, so dazzling that he couldn't see beyond his feet and his hand when he stretched his arm full length. He sat waiting for it to go out, but it didn't. The only sound was a drumming in his ears, but he began to imagine others, without knowing what they were – only knowing that he had cause to fear them. Was it imagination? He strained his ears but kept his eyes tightly closed, as if that could keep out some of the light.

Then he felt himself grabbed on either side. Hands gripped his arms and hauled him to his feet. He was thrust forward. He thought that he was going towards the door, but wasn't sure, the light had blinded him. He turned right and left, as they pushed him. Their grip hurt, but that wasn't important, only the blindness mattered; it was as if his eyes had suffered some permanent injury. His feet wouldn't go where he wanted them to, he stumbled, would have fallen but for the grip of the invisible men. They dragged instead of pushed him, the toes of his shoes scraped along a hard surface. He could hear the sound – and could also hear the footsteps of the men. Neither of them spoke.

He was dragged up a flight of stairs.

They stopped.

He was pulled upright and then thrust forward, staggered helplessly and crashed down. A sound behind him might have been the slamming of a door; another, the turning of a key. He didn't try to get up at once, but lay there, mouth wide open, gasping for breath. He still couldn't see, but there were curious shapes twisting and turning in front of his eyes, like the filament of giant electric lamps. At last he sat up; then stood up. The whirling shapes were smaller, less clearly defined, and he could tell the difference between light and darkness now. It was only a question of waiting. His legs felt stiff and painful, and he could feel the bruises where the powerful fingers had gripped his arms. He moved his hands vaguely. Finding only space, he took a few steps forward and moved them again. This time he touched something. A chair. He moved round it cautiously until he could safely sit down.

What would happen next?

Not light and darkness, for there was light in the room; he was recovering, and could see the wall – pictures on the wall, too. Silly pictures – that elephant, for instance. Who on earth would have a picture of an elephant, trunk curled upwards, as decoration? There were several other blurred shapes near it. He stood up slowly and concentrated on them, and they began to make sense – an inverted kind of sense. A giraffe, long neck stretched full length; a snarling lion, a tiger, a bear. The *Zoo*. This was crazy. Who would decorate walls with —

His thoughts seemed to be cut off.

After a moment of numbed horror he accepted the answer to that last question. Parents would decorate walls with animals – for their children. In their childhood Richard and Martin had woven wonderful stories about the animal faces stuck on the walls of their nursery.

These murals ran along the full length of one wall, and he

looked round, turned his head – and then stopped short. Tension as great as that he had felt beneath the flashing light came back to him.

In the corner behind him was a bed, and on the bed lay a child.

° ° °

The child was pale, about Ricky Shawn's size, with the same thin features. Was it Ricky Shawn? Who else would it be? The child was thinner than Roger remembered him from the photograph, but his eyes were enormous – rounded, terrified as he lay on the pillows. His arms were over the sheets; there was a steel bracelet round each wrist, and the bracelets were fastened by slender steel chains to the bed, so that the boy couldn't move. He couldn't speak, either. Adhesive plaster smothered his lips, a pink smear where the mouth ought to be. His nostrils were moving spasmodically as he breathed, his chest was heaving. The terror in his eyes was an ugly thing.

Roger moistened his lips, and tried to speak. He only croaked. He smiled, and knew that he must look grotesque, was frightening the boy still more. How could he offer reassurance? He took a step forward, and the child cringed back. He stopped and touched the chair, then slowly turned it to face the boy, and sat down. He swallowed the lump in his throat, waited until his mouth was moist, and then spoke.

'I – won't – hurt – you.'

The terror didn't fade, and there was no change in the boy's expression. Roger tried again, with the same words. It was no good. He doubted if the child heard him. He stood up, slowly, and repeated:

'I won't hurt you.'

He went towards the small bed, and again the boy cringed back, but this time Roger went on until he was at the side of the bed. He smiled down, and this time his lips didn't curl into grotesque lines; this time it was a more natural smile. He had to reassure the child; it wasn't a question of trying, he had to do it. He put his right hand out and touched the boy's forehead, smoothed it gently and smiled again. He didn't think it did any good. The small forehead was cold as marble. Cold – and the room was warm.

'I'll try to help you,' Roger said. He couldn't make a promise, one never made a promise to a child unless it could be kept. 'I'll try. Do you feel all right?'

The rounded eyes peered into his, still with no easing of the terror, no relaxing. The little arms, bare nearly to the elbow, were pale but taut. Roger moved away, pulled the chair up and sat near the bed. There was no indication that the boy heard him, nothing had yet penetrated that cruel shell of terror.

'Listen to me,' Roger said slowly. 'Nod if you can hear me. Nod your head if you can hear me.' He paused. 'Can you hear me?'

He waited, feeling a surge of helplessness, and then won a slight reward. The boy nodded slowly, twice. Was it imagination, or was there at last a slight easing of the intensity of his fear?

'That's good,' said Roger. 'Nod if you understand me. I am going to try to get you away from here. Do you understand?'

A pause; then another nod.

'And a lot of people are trying to find you. Your mother and father – a lot of other people, too. Do you understand?'

A nod.

Roger said: 'Have they hurt you, Ricky?' He wanted to pull off the plaster, but before he started, he had to win the boy's confidence. Even if he started, would he be allowed to finish? 'Have they hurt you, Ricky?'

The door opened, the boy's gaze switched and the terror

flared up again. Roger turned as a man said:

'We haven't hurt him, yet. We haven't hurt *you*, yet. Get up and come with me.'

16

QUESTIONS

He was a short man with broad shoulders, stocky, alert. His dark hair was brushed off a forehead which hadn't a wrinkle. His features were small in a big face – his mouth a puppet's mouth. He wore only trousers and a shirt, and a tie that was pulled away from his neck, and looked fresh and cool. He didn't show a gun, and the bigger man behind him in the doorway had empty hands.

The stocky man gripped Roger's arm, waking the bruises to protest, but he didn't resist – resistance wouldn't get him anywhere. Not yet. He didn't look round at the child again. He was pushed to the right at the passage, and still in that powerful grip, hustled to the end of it and then through an open door. The passage wasn't long, and there was ample room for two men to walk side by side.

Beyond the door a flight of wooden steps led downwards. He went down between the two men, turned right into a kitchen which glistened with white tiles and steel fittings, crossed a small room which had an arched doorway but no door, and then found himself in a long, narrow room, subdued lights, easy chairs, and all the furniture of a pleasant lounge, making it look homely and comfortable.

Sitting in an armchair at the far end of the room, legs stretched out, head resting against the back of the chair, was Gissing. And Gissing smiled at him.

There wasn't any possibility of a mistake.

Here were the dark eyes, with almost hairless brows, and short, stunted lashes, the long, pale face and narrow, pointed chin, the small hooked nose and the thin gash of a mouth. Gissing was relaxed, smiling as if amused. This time he wore cotton gloves, and not adhesive plaster; he wasn't going to leave fingerprints anywhere.

'Come and sit down, West,' he said.

The big man pushed Roger forward. He steadied himself against the side of a table, watching Gissing. An easy chair with its back to a draped window stood across the room, and he went across to it and sat down. He didn't look round, but was sure that the men who had brought him from the boy's room were still in the doorway. Then he forgot them. Gissing's voice, so much more pleasant than his looks, was calm and amiable – he seemed genial, as if he were a world removed from the blinding lights and the captive child.

'Bring Mr West a drink, Mac.'

Mac for McMahon, who had taken a boy aboard an aircraft?

The stocky man with the big face and small features came forward; Roger hadn't visualized him at a cocktail cabinet.

'Whisky and soda,' Gissing said. 'You haven't been here long enough to acquire new tastes, have you?'

'I've exactly the same likes and dislikes as always,' Roger said. He hoped his smile wasn't too sickly.

Gissing chuckled.

'And you don't like me! There's no need to get hot about it, but you're not a man to blow your top, are you? The drink is all right this time, although the one at the Milton Hotel wasn't.'

So he hadn't been brought here to be offered the poisoned cup. Gissing wanted to talk, to question him. Roger took the whisky and soda, and sipped. He could have emptied the glass in a gulp, and called for more, but resisted the impulse. He put it on a small table by his side, where a box of cigarettes and a lighter stood. He took a cigarette, lit it, and looked at Gissing.

'Where do you think this is going to get you?'

'Just where I want to go,' said Gissing, and laughed comfortably. The contrast between his manner and his looks was still startling. Had Roger been blindfolded, he would have got the impression of a mild-mannered, friendly man who amused himself with nothing more deadly than playing hit songs from popular and rather dated musicals. 'The boy hasn't been hurt, West. He was chained to the bed and plastered just to impress you. Not with what we've done, but with what we can do. I don't want to hurt the kid. *He's* done nothing.'

'So you're a humanitarian, too,' Roger said. 'It'll take years to repair the damage you've done to his mind.'

'Quite the psychiatrist,' Gissing said sarcastically. 'I didn't bring you here to talk about him, though. Why did you come to New York, West?'

'On an assignment.'

'To identify me?'

'I can't stop you guessing.'

'No,' Gissing said softly. 'You can't stop me from guessing. You can't prevent yourself from talking, either.' He shifted his position a little, but still relaxed, legs stretched out and hands resting on the arms of his chair. He wasn't drinking or smoking. 'You can have it the easy way, or you can have it the hard way. You're on special assignment, to find me. You're working with Marino, which makes you a man of importance. You're going to tell me how much Marino knows. Nothing will help you, if you don't. I want to know how long Marino has been watching me, who else he knows in my set-up, everything. Take it the easy way, West. If you talk, you won't get hurt. I'm leaving soon, you won't know where to look for me – no one will. You won't be able to do me any harm, and I've nothing against you. I don't want to hurt you any more than I want to hurt the boy. Don't be difficult, just tell me everything you know about the Shawn case – just how much Marino has told you.'

Roger didn't answer.

Gissing said without raising his voice: 'I'm not a patient man, and it won't trouble me if they hurt you. It wouldn't worry me to hear you screaming, and if I saw your fingers bent and broken and your mouth a mash of blood where they'd pulled your teeth with pinchers, it wouldn't lose me any sleep. It would be a waste of a good policeman, and I don't like waste if it can be avoided. Just talk.' He smiled, sat up, and raised a hand.

The stocky man in the doorway moved forward. Roger felt tension rising, the stealthy movement did more to work upon his fears than loud-voiced threats. He didn't move or look round, but expected a blow; instead, Mac came in front of him with another whisky and soda. He put it down next to Roger's half-empty glass and went away.

'You can have as much as you like of whatever you like,' Gissing said. 'You'll be comfortable and well fed. We'll have to hold you for a few weeks, but that's all. McMahon and Jaybird will take care of you.'

But these two men had been in London.

'Just tell me what you know,' Gissing added.

Roger took the first glass, sipped, looked over the top of it into the face which seemed as if it were naked, and said:

'Shawn is doing valuable work which he can only do in England, but I know no details. Marino believes that some-one is very anxious to get him back here. Kidnapping the boy and bringing him over here would do that. Marino didn't know that you were involved. The Yard got on to you by tracing the car, then getting the Paris police to see Mrs Norwood. The Paris police connected her with you, because of the recent suspected smuggling.'

'Go on.'

'We found out that Scammel worked for you, so did a man named Jaybird. We found Scammel's body less than twelve hours after the kidnapping. That's the job you'll pay for.'

Gissing waved his hand, as if it wasn't worth a thought.

'You don't have to tell me how good you are at the Yard, I'll take it as read. Marino went to the Yard, and you were assigned to help him. And Marino told you the story.'

Roger was glad of the whisky; his mouth kept going dry.

'Marino told me that we had to get the boy back, and try to keep Shawn in England.'

Gissing didn't speak, just looked; and his eyes narrowed, the faint lines of the smile faded.

'He wanted the whole business kept secret, and I said we hadn't a chance of getting results if it were. He lost too much time before releasing the story.'

'Or I was too quick,' Gissing said, mildly. 'If the story had been released twelve hours earlier, it wouldn't have made any difference. We had the boy here, and we've got Shawn back in the country. He's going to stay. Get on with it, West. I'm not interested in the mechanics of the investigation. I want to know what Marino told you about – whoever is anxious to get Shawn back. How much does he know?'

'If he knows anything, he didn't tell me.'

'So he didn't,' Gissing said softly. His face lost every hint of amiability, became vicious. 'You've got a bad memory.'

'If he knows anything, he didn't tell me.'

'He just sent you here for a pleasant little vacation?'

'You know the answer to that one,' Roger said. 'He hoped that they'd trace you over here, and I could identify you.'

Gissing laughed, and this time his laugh did nothing to give Roger an easy mind. It was hot, so hot that Gissing took off his gloves. He leaned further back in his chair.

'I know about that. You're the only man here who could point a finger and say "That is the man who talked to David Shawn." Now he can't find you, and so he can't identify me.

You didn't find a fingerprint or anything that would help at 'Rest' – I hadn't been there for weeks. Clarice won't talk, and no one else can – no one would rat on me. That puts you on a hook, but you can climb off it. You can have a long vacation, up in these hills, and when it's all over and I've gone, you can go back to your wife and family. You're like Shawn, quite the family man. But first, you have to tell me what Marino told you.'

'I've told you all he told me.'

Gissing's right hand strayed to the table by his side. Absently – or was it absently? – he picked up a paper-knife; all that betrayed his tension beneath the cloak of calm. He had put prints on that knife and it became a vital thing. He nursed the knife. His dark eyes held no expression. His lips were set tightly. Slowly he began to smile.

'You do understand, don't you, West? I'm going to get that story. If you have to be smashed up before you'll talk, it is not going to worry me. But sooner or later you are going to talk.'

'There isn't a thing more I can tell you,' Roger declared flatly.

Insisting on that was a waste of time. Everything was a waste of time. They would set to work on him and they would know their job, it was going to be hell. He hadn't even reached the stage of thinking about escape. He simply felt fear creeping into him, driving away the warm glow from the whisky. Then he had a wild idea – 'escape' came to him as a word; escape and the desire to hurt Gissing. The man wouldn't expect —

Gissing had hurtled Shawn away from him, without effort. Gissing would never be unprepared, and two silent, powerful men were a few feet away. The only hope he had was to use persuasion, trying to make Gissing believe what he didn't want to believe. He wouldn't succeed by raising his voice, if there were a chance it would come by holding himself steady, behaving as Gissing behaved.

He shrugged.

'Now let's have the story, West.'

'There isn't a story,' Roger said. 'You'll only waste your time. I can't get away so I can't identify you, you've drawn my teeth already.' He actually managed a smile. 'You're good at kidnapping, you might be luckier next time.'

Gissing's eyes narrowed, he weighed the paper-knife in his hands; pale hands, well shaped, well tended; the nails were filmed with colourless varnish.

'I'm lucky this time,' he said.

'You just think you're lucky.'

Gissing put the knife down and stood up, slowly. He drew nearer. He was close enough for Roger to reach with his foot. One kick, and he would stagger away, but – two pairs of eyes were watching.

Gissing looked down; from this angle his expression was vicious.

'West, I am the man who kidnapped the boy, and had Scammel killed. Jaybird, just behind you, followed Shawn to Barnes to make sure he wasn't leading the police there. He saw those detectives who took too much notice of Shawn, and he ran them down. The other man behind you brought the boy here. That is how tough we are.'

'I still can't tell you anything more.'

'If you don't know, who does?' Gissing asked, and kept his voice casual.

Roger shrugged.

'Who does?' repeated Gissing, and he spoke as if Roger wasn't in the room, seemed to have lost interest. 'I have to find out what Marino knows, now. Who can tell me? Lissa Meredith?'

The name came questioningly and was an obvious guess. Roger, half prepared for it, showed no reaction, but his heart leapt; could *she* be in the kind of danger he was in now?

'I don't think so,' he answered. 'She said Marino kept her in the dark. She just has to try to calm Shawn down.'

'Would she tell you what she knew?' Gissing asked flatly. It was almost as if he were convinced that Roger had told the truth. *Could* he be? No, it was too easy, he was fooling, he would switch back to threat and menace in a moment. 'Maybe not. What about Carl Fischer?'

'Who?'

'*Doctor* Fischer.'

'Oh,' said Roger. 'I don't know much about him. He's a friend of Shawn's as well as a doctor attached to the Embassy.'

'Attached nothing, he's over here with Shawn now. Carl Fischer and the Meredith girl are trying to smooth him down, hoping to get him back to England. They haven't a chance. Do you think they have a chance?'

'I wouldn't know.'

Roger wished the man would move, wished the stare from those dark eyes wasn't so intense. He wanted to get up. Gissing crowded him, now. He was inviting an assault. It would be easy. A toecap cracking against his knee, a spring, a savage blow over the head, but – two men standing in the doorway.

Then a bell rang, blasting the quiet. It was no ordinary bell, but a harsh, strident warning. It made Gissing back away and swing round, it made the two men exclaim, it gave Roger a chance he wasn't likely to get again. The bell wrenched their thoughts away from him, put alarm into them.

McMahon and Jaybird leapt out of sight.

17

DARK NIGHT

It was only a lightning flash of time. Gissing stared at the doorway, the bell clanging, the men scrambling towards another door – then he moved back, his right hand dropped to his pocket, he actually started to say:

'Don't mo —'

Roger slid forward in his chair, hooked the man's feet from under him, sent him crashing. Gissing's hand came from his pocket, the side that lay uppermost. Farther away, footsteps sounded like a stampede. Gissing lashed out with his foot, his hand went back to his pocket. Roger snatched at the ankle as the foot swung past him, caught hold, heaved Gissing's leg backwards. The man gasped with pain. Roger let him go, bent down and knocked the hand away from his pocket. Gissing hadn't any fight left.

Roger's fingers touched cold steel. He drew out the gun. He saw Gissing's face twisted, heard only the man's harsh breathing, but knew the other threat might return. He turned the gun in his hand, struck Gissing on the base of the skull, heard the soughing breath as unconsciousness came. He turned the gun again, looked towards the doorway, and saw the drapes move.

He fired.

The bullet tore through the drapes, a man grunted and pitched forward into sight.

Throughout all this the bell was still clanging.

The falling man had a gun in his right hand but no control over it. Roger went forward. The gun fell at his feet, and he kicked it away. The man hit the floor with a heavy thud, and didn't move. He wouldn't move again by himself, Roger knew. He must have been crouching, and the bullet had hit him in the temple. It was a small, clean hole, and the blood hadn't started to ooze out.

Gissing unconscious, a dead man, and the helpless boy downstairs.

Suddenly the bell stopped. It was as if agonizing pressure had been eased from Roger's ears.

If he could get that boy —

He heard a shot, and thought it came from outside. Footsteps thudded, their sound dulled by the closed windows; then more footsteps, nearer now and coming from the rooms through which Roger had been brought. Two men at least were approaching, and luck couldn't last. He opened a door at the far end of the room. Another, just a gauze-filled wooden frame, was immediately beyond it. The footsteps drew nearer inside the house, farther away outside. Roger unhooked the catch of the outer door, and found himself on a wide verandah lit only by the light from the room.

He heard a shout: 'Get him!' A shot barked from behind him, and he heard the bullet bite into the door-frame. He swung right, jumped down the verandah steps and rushed towards the beckoning darkness. More shots barked as he raced blindly over the grass, but he wasn't hit. Against the grey sky he could see the dark outline of the spiked tops of trees. Some way off these trees offered shelter. His footsteps seemed to thump out a call. *'Here I am, here I am.'* He could hear the others running, and looked up at the tops of the trees and wondered how far away they were, and whether he could reach them. He was breathing hard, but didn't feel panic, just unnatural calm. Then he heard two more shots, farther away, and out of the corner of his eye he saw the flashes. He was running at right angles to that spot.

Brushing against a bush, he felt a branch hard against his shoulder, and ducked; another branch plucked at his hair. So he had reached the trees. He sensed rather than saw the straight trunks and the low branches. The men behind him were blundering through the undergrowth. They hadn't gathered their wits yet, but soon they would use flashlights. He stopped running and walked on swiftly. A murmur of voices came from behind him, and then there was a shout from a long way off – where the last shooting had been. A shout of triumph?

He could see a little now, stopped and turned round. The light from the house, two hundred yards away at least, showed up the trees in silhouettes, and he saw he was in a small thicket. Between him and the house there were rows of young firs, then trees with taller, thicker trunks. Against the glow he saw a man appear from the house, running towards the thicket, light coming from his flashlight. With a powerful light they had a chance of finding him; and they knew where they were, what the ground was like. Roger moved cautiously, wondering whether caution would help him. He walked parallel with the edge of the turf and the first line of young trees, until the man with the flashlight was within a hundred yards. Then he turned towards the grass – the old gambit, doubling back; nothing else could help him.

Other flashlights were shining, on the far side of the turf. He stared towards them, fancying that one man was being dragged along by two others; a third and a fourth, lighting the way, were in the party. Then he heard the man coming towards the thicket call out:

'See him?'

'This way.'

They were heading for the spot where Roger had first disappeared into the trees. He reached the grass, then turned again and walked along the edge of the thicket away from the house, the light of which was now too far away to show him up. The shadowy darkness of the trees hid him.

One party with their prisoner was going towards the

house, the other was looking for Roger in the wrong place. Grant him just a little luck, and he *would* get away. A little more still, and he would find a telephone and get help, bring a rescue party to the house in time to save the boy, perhaps catch Gissing.

How had that alarm been raised?

The grounds might be ringed with a trip-wire; or a gate protected with an alarm. Did it matter? Someone had blundered into the alarm system, and been caught; it didn't seem to matter who. Roger quickened his step, sure that there was no immediate danger. He could no longer hear the men who were seeking him.

He could see much better now. Another row of trees was facing him; the trees seemed to grow completely round the grounds with the house built in a clearing. It was downhill, here – the big disadvantage was that he didn't know what the ground would be like a few steps ahead. There was a danger of running round in circles, too. He mustn't hurry, he must keep his bearings.

There were no stars.

He looked for a light, other than the lights at the house and those from the flashlights, but saw nothing. He had his back to the house, and the glow from that would shine for a long way, if he kept his back to it he could at least be sure that he was getting farther away.

The trees were thinning.

The ground was even but slippery with pine-needles; he couldn't go too fast. The immediate danger was past, but any mistakes now could damn him. If he were taken back, he wouldn't find a smooth-voiced Gissing, he would find a devil.

He kicked against something that struck his ankle, and then heard a sound – a long way off, like the ringing of a bell. It went on and on. He glanced over his shoulder. The flashlights had stopped moving towards the house. He felt sweat breaking out. This was the trip-wire, the alarm had gone off again. He hadn't a knife, couldn't break it. He didn't try, but began to run along it, then realized that if the wire ran round the clearing, they wouldn't know whereabouts it had been touched again. He climbed over, and ran on.

Were there guards?

He had taken it for granted that everyone in the grounds had gone towards the man who was now a prisoner, but he must not take that or anything else for granted.

He stopped running, and now and again looked over his shoulder. The light from the house fell away to a dim glow, well above him, and the hillside was much steeper. Twice, he nearly pitched forward. The trees were all about him. He looked round again, and the light had vanished, but by going downhill he could be sure that he was getting farther away. His legs felt stiff and heavy, his back ached and his head throbbed. He hadn't been aware of any of that at first, now he had time to think of it; and it became an obsession – that, and the need for keeping out of the way of the men who would be searching. If he had any idea where to go, it would have given him hope, but this was an unknown wilderness. There was no light anywhere, only the greyness of the sky and the darkness of the trees.

He stumbled on.

He didn't know how long the transition took, but after a while he stopped thinking clearly, stopped being afraid of pursuit, somehow dragged one foot in front of the other and made himself go forward. He had no watch. He had no sense of time. Now his whole body ached, every muscle seemed to groan in protest. There was a sharp pain at the back of his right foot, another where he had kicked against the wire, but he knew that he must go on, and clung to that, forcing his feet to carry him farther. After a while, he knew that he would soon have to stop, that it would soon be impossible to keep moving. Each leg seemed like a leaden weight. The sharper pains were worse. His head now throbbed as badly as it had done after the blow at 'Rest'. His mouth was wide open and he was gasping uncontrollably.

The hillside was behind him, he was on level ground now. Gradually he became aware of something different, as if his feet were being clawed back into the earth. He had taken a dozen floundering steps before he realized that he was walking through marshland. That set a new conscious fear flaring into his mind. Marshes – bog. God! Where was he? Why didn't he come to a road?

He didn't come to a road.

He came to a clearing in the trees. A long way off there was light – light of all colours, tiny bars of green and blue and red and yellow. So far off that they were as far away as the stars. He stopped and swayed, putting one hand against a tree for support, then leaned against the tree. Water was up to his ankles. He studied the lights, and slowly the truth dawned. This was a lake. The patch of treeless darkness ahead was the smooth surface of the water. On the other side, miles away, was a village.

He was still breathing through his mouth.

He made himself think. The lights seemed to be directly opposite him, but he couldn't judge which was the quicker way round. Right or left? He could turn in the wrong direction and never get there. This might be one lake or a string of lakes. There was no means of telling, he had to take a chance. So, woodenly, he turned right.

Sand and water were underfoot. He could hear the soft rippling of the water, which was cold at first, and slowly became icy. Trees grew right to the water's edge nearly everywhere, now and again they receded and he could walk on dry ground, but the stretches were never long. The lights seemed to be just as far away, and he was haunted by the fear that this lake would run into another, and that he couldn't reach that village. There was no light in front of him, no gleam that offered hope.

He came to a clearing.

He took Gissing's gun from his pocket, went a few feet away from the water and plodded on, but tremors ran through his legs, they wouldn't support him much longer.

A pain stabbed so sharply that he called out, and paused.

It would be easy to stop, to sit down, to stretch out, to rest. He longed to make the sand of the water's edge a couch. He stared downwards all the time, and yet he didn't see the boat. He kicked against it, barked his shin, and fell. The gun dropped from his hand and plopped into water; was lost for good. A tree-stump? A rock? A fallen branch? He looked, and saw the dark outline of the small boat – long, canoe-like. The handle of a paddle stuck up.

He thought dully: 'A boat. A *boat*.' He turned his head to stare at the inviting lights. Were they nearer or farther away?

He had a *boat*.

He saw something that seemed to grow out of the calm water; a small landing-stage. A boat and a landing-stage meant that someone often came here, might *live* here. He turned his head slowly, and made out the shape of a building, not big, but standing dark and solid against the trees. A building, but no light.

He turned towards it, less acutely conscious of the burden of his body. He did not expect to find anyone here. The door would be locked and the windows securely fastened – unless whoever lived here was asleep. He called out, but his voice was only a croak. He called again, and knew that it would be difficult to hear the sound more than a few yards away. He reached the side of the building, and banged, but had no strength to thump. The walls seemed to echo.

No one spoke, nothing happened.

He moved towards the left, where the hut faced the lake,

and kicked against steps which led – where else could they lead? – to a front door. There was no rail. He mounted the steps unsteadily. The door faced him, he pushed, and the door opened.

That was so unlikely, that he stopped swaying drunkenly, hand stretched out, door creaking as it swung away from him. An age passed before he stepped up, and into the hut. It was darker here than it had been outside. That ordeal had ended in an empty hut and a canoe he hadn't the strength to use, but he could rest. He must rest. There would be a chair, surely there would be a chair.

He started the cautious circling round the room; it seemed like second nature to walk with his hands outstretched. He felt rough wood walls, kicked nothing, began to think that it was empty of everything, and then his hand touched a shelf. He groped along it. Something moved. He explored it slowly, and knew that it was something cold, smooth and round. He gripped it as tightly as he could and took it off the shelf, and then he realized what it was – a flashlight.

Would it work?

18

'EMPTY' HOUSE

ROGER pressed the switch. There was no strength in his fingers, and it would not budge. He screwed himself up for the effort, and light came on. It shone into his eyes, and he jerked his head away. The beam wove a yellow pattern on walls and floor, before he held it still. He raised it towards the shelf. There was no sound but the creaking of boards beneath his feet, the light shone on some tins, rope, a hurricane lantern – then a rustle of movement made him swing round.

Before he saw what it was, a heavy weight struck his hand, knocking the torch from his grasp. It clattered to the floor and went out. Blackness – always blackness. His heart thumped and he felt suffocated.

They'd caught him.

'You looking for anything?' a man said laconically.

Roger opened his mouth, muttered a sound that must have seemed like gibberish. The man said:

'You heard me. What are you doing around here?'

Roger said slowly and carefully: 'I – am – lost.'

'That so?' The voice was still laconic. 'Just come to the door, friend. I'd like to take a look at you.'

The voice came from the door, but Roger could see nothing. He moved forward, a step at a time. A light shone into his eyes, not powerful enough to dazzle him. Then it dropped and a woman said:

'Mike, he's just another bum.'

'Looks like,' said Mike. The light travelled again to Roger's face. 'Looks like he's had a long walk, I guess. You a stranger to these parts?'

'I have just come —' the words seemed to hesitate before they came out – 'from England.' As if that would mean anything to them – except to suggest that he was lying.

'From England,' the woman echoed.

'That so?' Mike's voice had calmness in it and could have been friendly. 'Then you're a mighty long way from home.' He kept the light steady. 'Honey, you just step behind him and make sure he doesn't carry a gun.'

She moved without hesitating. After a moment, Roger felt her hands at his sides, patting his coat and trousers; she was thorough.

'No,' she said.

'Okay, stranger,' Mike said. 'You can come this way.' He began to move, just visible in the reflected light of the torch. The woman took Roger's arm, as if she realized his weakness.

He almost blacked out. He knew they were both helping to keep him on his feet. There was some trouble at a flight of steps before he stumbled inside a dimly lighted room and was lowered into a chair. He heard odd words. 'Coffee.' 'Looks mighty sick to me.' 'Don't wake them kids.' Kids. The boy!

He opened his eyes wide and started to speak, but Mike wouldn't let him. Mike was a big, hardy-looking man with a grey-streaked beard, wearing a lumber jacket of coloured squares, trousers held up by a silver-buckled belt and a pair of old boots. The room was small and two other rooms led off it. The woman had disappeared, but Roger could just distinguish the clink of china and it wasn't long before she came back with a percolator and cups on a tray. There were sandwiches as well as coffee. She poured out.

'Mike, you want to take his shoes off?'

'For why?'

'You want to use your eyes,' she said tartly. 'He's been wading in the lake.' She stirred sugar into the coffee and pushed cup and saucer into Roger's hands. 'Just you drink that, and then eat some, and then —'

'Thanks,' Roger said. 'I – thanks. But don't touch my shoes.' Mike was on one knee obediently. 'I've got to – go on. I must get to the police.'

Mike stopped moving, just stared up at him. His wife went still.

'I must telephone the police,' Roger said, as if he were repeating a lesson learned parrot-wise. 'There is a kidnapped boy.' He waved his left hand, nearly knocked the cup out of the saucer. 'Up there.'

Husband and wife looked at each other, looked back at Roger.

'There is,' he persisted. 'I must tell the police. How far away – are they?'

'State troopers in Wycoma,' Mike said, as if he were talking to himself. His wife was staring intently at Roger, but once looked towards the door she hadn't been through. 'The nearest telephone is six-seven miles, I guess. You sure about this boy?'

'Yes. We must hurry.'

'Where is he, you say?'

'Drink your coffee,' the woman ordered.

'Up there. A big house – in a clearing. Trees all round it. Firs – or pines.' The warm coffee was thawing Roger out, he felt more able to cope, and he was beginning to feel that these people might help. 'I don't know how far. Miles. It's at the top of a hill.'

Mike said: 'Webster's old place. Webster doesn't live there any more, since his boy died. Heard some funny stories about the guy who took over. So there's a kid. What's the name of the kid?'

'Shawn,' said Roger. 'Ricky Shawn. He was kidnapped in England —'

Mike moved quickly for the first time. On his way to the door, he said:

'You want to look after him while I'm gone, honey? Won't be that long. Could be the kid's up there, or could be this guy's crazy, but it won't do any harm to look and see. I'll telephone Wycoma, stranger, and be right back with the police.' He stopped in the doorway. 'I'm Mike Hill,' he said, and obviously expected a comment.

'You've been very —' Roger began, and stopped, forcing a smile. 'I'm Roger West. I'm not crazy. Hurry, Mike, please.'

Two minutes later, the quiet of the lakeside was broken by the stutter of a car engine. Soon it moved off, missing on one cylinder but chugging steadily. Mike Hill's wife was pouring more coffee and urging Roger to eat the sandwich: a chicken sandwich. The sound of the engine died away.

• • •

There were three New York State troopers in uniform, two other men, Mike Hill and Roger. Hill's old car was left by the lake, his wife stood in the doorway of the cabin, watching a big Pontiac and an Oldsmobile moving along the track towards a dirt road, head-lights carving a light through the trees. By road, Webster's place was fifteen miles away, Roger was told; he had walked nine. It was nearly four o'clock in the morning.

They had asked few questions, all seemed sleepy and taciturn. Now he matched their silence. His eyes were so heavy that sleep was always threatening him, and his limbs would not stop aching. He knew that they were in the Adirondacks about two hundred miles from New York City, that was all.

The narrow road twisted all the way, ran uphill, and on the hairpin bends there was hardly room for two cars to pass. The journey took them forty minutes.

It didn't surprise Roger that Webster's house was empty. Gissing, the boy, the new prisoner – all of them were gone. He forced himself to keep up with the others as they searched. Evidence of hurried departure, bullet marks in the floor and the door-frame, blood on the carpet where the man had died, told them he hadn't been lying. Of them all, the most morose was a lean, leathery man with a puckered dent in the side of his neck, from an old injury. The others called him Al, and he had a sergeant's stripes. They had finished the search and were back in the room where Roger had seen Gissing. Sergeant Al went towards the chair where Gissing had sat, looked at Roger with small shiny brown eyes, and said thinly:

'Now tell us just what happened, will you.'

'Al,' protested Mike Hill, 'the guy's dead on his feet.'

'I can use my eyes,' said Al. 'You keep out of this.' His hand strayed towards the table by Gissing's chair, near the paper-knife. 'Tell us what happened, going right back to —'

Roger snapped: 'Don't touch that! Don't touch that knife.'

Al snatched his hands away, as if the knife were red-hot. 'He handled it,' Roger said, and weariness and pain were wiped out in a flash of exhilaration. 'The kidnapper handled it, his prints are on it. Don't touch it. Don't let anyone else know you've got it.'

'Okay,' said Al, and smiled for the first time. 'You don't have to get excited. You want to get me an envelope,' he said to one of the others. 'Now, Mr West —'

He didn't finish. Someone by the front door called out that a man was approaching, Sergeant Al left Roger, three men went into the night – a night beginning with a false dawn to bring another day. There were voices in the distance. They drew nearer, and men came on to the verandah. Then another man was brought in, dishevelled, face scratched, clothes torn, exhausted – but recognizable through all that.

'Pullinger!' Roger exclaimed.

Pullinger looked as if he would have fallen but for the support of strong arms. He grinned weakly.

'Hi, Roger,' he said. 'You're a lucky guy. Let me sit down, and give me a drink. A big drink.' He grinned as the men led him to a chair, then slumped into it.

• • •

A bath, a shave and bacon and eggs, turned Roger from a wreck into a man again. He would be stiff for several days, but stiffness didn't matter. Pullinger had called him lucky, and he didn't argue. Pullinger couldn't complain, either.

He told his story to Sergeant Al and Roger, and refused to have anyone else present; a card he showed to Al won him all the necessary respect. After leaving Roger at the New York hotel, Pullinger had felt tired, without reason, and suspected dope, called a colleague and been picked up before he lost consciousness. His colleague had seen Roger half-carried out of the Milton Hotel, like a drunk. With an unconscious Pullinger beside him, the other FBI man followed the car through the night, but without a chance to stop to ask for help. On the Cross Country Parkway, he had been side-swiped by another car, which had gone on, allowing the first car to get well away. But Pullinger's man had kept going, and had caught up with and seen their quarry.

'It was a raid by ourselves, or lose you for good,' said Pullinger. Pullinger had come round in the early hours. They had stayed near the place where they had lost the car, and spotted it again the next evening, with Roger still in it. Roger had been unconscious for over twenty-four hours. The two men had then followed the car to Webster's old house and fallen foul of the trip wire.

'They caught Buddy,' Pullinger went on bleakly. 'I got away. I fell down a gully and into a creek, it seemed hours before I climbed out. I was just in time to see them streaking out of the house as if they had dynamite behind them. So I waited – but I didn't come too close. Then you arrived, but how was I to know that you were on my side?'

'That's okay, Mr Pullinger,' Sergeant Al said. 'Now you can take it easy. I called State Headquarters, and they called the New York Police Department, and if we have the luck, they won't get far away with that boy.'

Pullinger said: 'I could tear them apart with my own hands.' He looked down at his hands, but he didn't look at Roger.

They were in a hotel in Wycoma, with the remains of breakfast on a table between them, cigarette-stubs messy in a saucer, a vacuum cleaner humming not far away. Outside, the morning sun shone on the lake and the trees which lined its banks. Pullinger stood up.

'Now I'm going to get some sleep,' he declared. 'You too, Roger.'

'I've had all the sleep I want.'

'I told you you were a lucky guy! Right, then. The Sergeant will take you around. You and I will drive back to

New York later in the day, unless we get other orders.' He stifled a yawn. 'You're still the only man here who can put a finger on Gissing.'

'I won't forget him in a hurry,' Roger said.

'Sergeant,' said Pullinger, 'take good care of Mr West, he's precious.' He yawned again and went out of the room.

The door closed with a snap. Sergeant Al said he must be getting along, and looked into Roger's eyes, giving the impression that he was asking a question.

'Maybe you'll come with me, Mr West, because I need to put in a full report.'

'Why not,' agreed Roger.

The office wasn't far away. The wide main street of Wycoma was hard-topped, but the sidewalks were dusty. Few people were about. Big gleaming cars stood by parking meters or in garages. Two drug stores and a supermarket were half empty and Roger's gaze was drawn to the crowded shelves. Sergeant Al talked, economically. The season was nearly over, the weather would break any time, and then there wouldn't be much doing until spring. He led the way, nodding without speaking to several clerks and to one of the troopers who had been with him during the night. Reaching his office he ushered Roger inside, then closed the door. He opened a drawer in his desk and drew out the envelope containing the paper-knife.

'I did what you said, Mr West. But I can't give you this, I must hand it over to my boss. I ain't said a word to anyone about it, the other guys will keep quiet too.'

'The fewer people who know we have that man's prints the better,' said Roger.

He didn't know who he would see yet, and wasn't prepared to voice any doubts about Pullinger's story. He hadn't a lead, except through Pullinger, and he wanted one.

He could telephone Marino.

He *would* telephone Marino.

Al listened.

'Well,' Al said, and smiled again, 'I guess this may be the first call ever put through to England from Wycoma, Mr West, but that don't make any difference. But you could wait until you get to New York or Washington. Or else —'

He didn't finish.

That was because Roger heard a voice in the outer office, and was out of his chair and moving across the room quicker than he had thought he would be able to move for days. There was only one voice like that in the world. He reached the door in two strides, and pulled it open.

Lissa was saying to a trooper:

'Will I find Mr Roger West here? I was told —'

'Right here,' Roger said.

Lissa swung round, her eyes glowing. There was no sense in it, but it was like coming to the end of a journey.

19

SHAWN HOUSEHOLD

THEY didn't move or speak, their hands did not touch. They stood two yards from each other, Roger in the doorway with Sergeant Al behind him, Lissa oblivious of the trooper to whom she had just spoken and of the others now watching her. A girl stopped clattering on the typewriter, and silence fell. It could only have been for a few seconds, but it seemed age-long.

Sergeant Al, his little eyes bright, made a sound which might have meant anything, and broke the spell. As Roger relaxed, pictures of Janet and the boys flashed into his mind. But he felt no sense of guilt or even disquiet; it was as if emotion had been drawn out of him, leaving a strange emptiness that was both buoyant and satisfying.

'Hi, Roger,' Lissa said, and they gripped hands. 'You had me worried.'

'I was worried myself,' Roger said, and turned, still holding her hand. 'This is Sergeant Al.'

'Just Al?' Lissa's radiance brought a reluctant curve to the Sergeant's lips.

'Sergeant Al Ginney, ma'am.'

'I'm Lissa Meredith,' said Lissa.

All three went into the smaller office, and the Sergeant motioned to chairs and sat down himself, but Lissa continued to stand.

'I can't wait to hear everything. Roger, is it true that you've seen Ricky?'

He nodded.

'How – how was he?' She seemed almost afraid to ask.

'Frightened,' Roger told her, 'but not hurt.'

'You'll just *have* to see the Shawns. They're – they're worse even than you would expect. David thought that Ricky would be sent back once he came over here. Belle raves at him like a crazy woman. I don't want to get any nearer hell than that household.' She paused. 'Did you see *him* again?'

'Yes.'

'What's happening up there?' Lissa asked. 'Washington called me and said Ed Pullinger had arrived, too. I don't know the whole story yet.' She glanced at Al Ginney. 'Have you had instructions from Washington, Al?'

'No, ma'am. I would get them through Albany, anyway,' the Sergeant told her. 'But I guess I don't need instructions to do what Mr Pullinger says, and he says to let Mr West do anything he pleases.'

'Where is Mr Pullinger?'

'In bed. I guess he had a pretty hard time.'

'Do you know what happened to him in New York – and to you?' Lissa asked Roger.

'He told me about it.'

'Then we needn't disturb him,' Lissa decided. 'We'll drive to the Shawns' place at once. There isn't a thing more you can do here. Are you ready?'

'There's one little thing,' Roger said. 'That paper-knife, Sergeant.'

When he told her of the significance of the knife, she opened her handbag and took out a folded card; Roger saw that this had her photograph on it.

'We'll take that knife, Al,' she said.

Ginney studied the card, then studied her.

'Sure can, ma'am. I've taken the prints off it, they're on the record, and I've sent copies to New York by special messenger and to Washington by air. Mr West thinks they might be that important. There's a funny thing, Mr West. We've men up at Webster's old house, but haven't found another set of those same prints. We don't know for sure, but we think the man who left them on the knife arrived only an hour or so before Mr West got away.

'He wore gloves,' Roger said. 'He always wore gloves or had his fingers taped. He forgot himself for ten minutes, and that was enough.' Having the prints, knowing there were no others, heightened his sense of buoyancy. 'I'm ready when you are, Lissa.'

'What's holding us back?'

He shook hands with Al Ginney, who stepped with them to the street. A Cadillac convertible, wine-red cellulose and chromium glistening, stood in the shade of a spreading beech tree. By now more people were in the main street and in the shops. Most of the weather-board houses were freshly painted, looking bright and new. Only a cluster of shops had two storeys or more, while all the houses were the English bungalow type, but looked much larger.

Lissa took the wheel, and Ginney waved them off. Soon they passed the open doors of the little hotel where Roger had feasted on ham and eggs. Looking between the houses on the left, Roger caught glimpses of the lake; of trees on the lake shore, a brighter green than those farther from the water; of small craft moving slowly, an outboard motor-boat flashed past them with a stuttering roar. The far bank of the lake, where Roger had stood and looked at the lights of Wycoma during the night, now seemed much nearer. Beyond, hills rose in wooded slopes, and beyond the hills, peaks which looked like mountains.

Now he and Lissa were passing the end of a dirt road, and as they did so, a big car which had been standing there slid after them.

'See that?' Roger asked quietly.

'We're well guarded,' Lissa said. 'Someone thinks you're worth taking care of.'

Roger didn't speak.

'How do you feel?' asked Lissa.

'Stiff in places, otherwise I'm all right.'

'If you were half dead, you'd call yourself all right.'

She didn't look at him. The hood was down, wind sang past the windscreen and whipped round it, playing with her hair where it escaped the peaked pull-on cap she was wearing. He hadn't given much thought to her clothes before. The cap, wine red like the Cadillac, a beige shirt with large breast pockets, and a wine red skirt; simple, perfect for her. As she drove, she looked as if she held the secret of life.

'How far is it?' Roger asked.

'Say a hundred and sixty miles; we'll arrive late this afternoon.'

'How did you get here so soon?'

'I flew,' she said simply. 'The car was sent from Albany.'

'They look after you well.'

'They know how important this is, Roger,' Lissa said. 'Anyway they don't want anything else to happen to an English policeman over here! The fingerprints will help, but you're still the man who matters. The man who matters,' she repeated softly, and glanced at him. Then she laughed. 'It's too bad. You don't have two hours in New York before you get carried off, and even when you see the Adirondacks, you're being hunted or hustled. We're on the eastern slopes,' she went on. 'In a month or six weeks, you ought to come back to see the autumn leaves. I don't think there is anything like their colours in the world.' She laughed again, as if she were excited, and talked swiftly, as if anxious to stop herself from thinking too much. 'You'll have heard that too often already, Ed Pullinger couldn't help himself talking about New York. Do we talk too much about America? I often wish I knew just what the English think about us. Is it too bad?'

Roger said easily: 'I'd rather work with Marino than with most men I know.'

'Thank you.' She took her right hand off the wheel and rested it for a moment on Roger's knee. 'If there's one thing I want, it's that you should think well of us.'

He didn't have to tell her that he knew she meant it.

She drove fast without being reckless, and the other car was always in sight behind them. The first hour was through winding tree-clad slopes, hiding large lakes, allowing only occasional glimpses of them through the folds in the hills and the valleys. There was little traffic. The surface of the road was good, the edges roughly finished to eyes used to the neatness of English roads. Roger didn't consciously compare them, but sat back and let reflections drift in and out of his mind in a strange contentment. The aching in his limbs had eased, and now only the abrasions at his ankle and the back of his right heel stung, but not severely.

Soon they reached open land, pasture with long, wide vistas, and here it would have been easy to imagine that he was in an unfamiliar part of England. Only the big cars and the huge trucks were different; and the small towns, with their frame houses, each house surrounded by sweeping lawns and shaded from the hot sun by tall trees.

It was in one of those towns that they stopped for lunch, choosing a large, single-storey restaurant, where green blinds were down to keep out the sun, and a huge sign proclaimed:

Steaks
Chicken in the Basket
Boston Baked Beans

Roger hadn't eaten a bigger steak for years.

The big room was cool, the service friendly, music came from juke boxes fed with nickels by a family with three children who were sprawling over the chairs and examining the colourful candy-stand with eager eyes.

Afterwards, Lissa drove on tirelessly. They said little. Roger thought less, his mind a vacuum which he knew would soon have to be filled; but there was no need to fill it yet. Just after four o'clock they turned off a wide main road on to a narrow one with a good tar surface, and Lissa said:

'In another two miles, we'll be there. Roger, please try to help David. I know you don't like him, but try to help. I don't think – I don't think anyone could do anything to help Belle, unless it's David. That's why he needs all the help anyone can give him.'

'I'll try,' Roger promised. 'Has there been any ransom demand yet?'

'I forgot you didn't know. He paid some as soon as he got here. One hundred thousand dollars. When we found out he had cashed such a big cheque we made him talk, we got tough for once.' She didn't smile. 'He put it in an old chest in the house, and doesn't know who took it, although it must have been someone with access to the household.'

Roger nodded; looked at her; and wondered.

• • •

The house was in the old Colonial style, built of weatherboard, with tall round pillars at the front, on either side of the large verandah and the dozen steps leading up to it. It stood in parkland. Gardeners were working on the lawns and in the flower gardens, which were massed with colour. Hissing sprays of water filmed the air in a dozen places. On one side was a swimming-pool, with diving-board and two small brick-built sheds, one at each end. The water looked limpid in the sunshine, and shone pale blue because of the tiles.

Lissa pulled up at the front steps. The other car drove past them towards garages which were just visible. As they walked towards the open front door, Dr Carl Fischer appeared, a hand raised, face twisted in a smile. It might have been the direct rays of the sun, but it looked to Roger as if Fischer were showing signs of great strain.

He shook hands with Roger.

'They tell me you've been getting around.'

Roger smiled. 'A little,' he conceded.

'I'm glad you don't look like another patient,' said Fischer dryly.

'How are they?' Lissa asked as they entered the shady hall.

'Much worse, since they heard that Ricky had been traced and lost again. The news came over the radio, someone must have picked it up in Wycoma.' Fischer glanced at Roger almost accusingly, as if to blame him for the news leaking out. 'Belle gave David another look at hell after that. He looks as if he's turning into stone, I don't think he's slept since he got back. He won't have a shot. I can't give Belle any more, she's built up a resistance.'

'I'd better go and see her,' Lissa said almost wearily. 'Where is she?'

'In her room. I shouldn't go yet, she's quiet. When she sees Roger, she'll blow up again.' Fischer had as much time for Belle Shawn as he would have for a dog with rabies, if his manner were any guide. 'David's in the library.' He stopped by an open door. 'I won't come with you, if you don't mind. I could use some sleep myself.'

'You go and rest,' Lissa said.

Fischer was obviously so tired that he could have gone to sleep on his feet.

As he went upstairs with Lissa, Roger glanced at her, wondering how much of the brightness of her eyes was due to over-exhaustion. It was hard to believe that she, too, hadn't slept, but if this household were as she had said, and Fischer had confirmed this, how could she have done so? Yet she had shown no sign of fatigue on the journey, had been bright-eyed when she had come to Sergeant Al's office. Perpetual youth? Roger found himself scowling at his own strange fancy and stranger mood.

Now they were on a spacious landing, oil paintings, mostly portraits, on the walls, the floors highly polished, skin rugs showing up darkly against the light brown of the wood. Lissa went straight to a door on the left, the farthest from the staircase, opened it and went straight in. As she glanced back, her look said:

'Wait, Roger.'

He waited.

She walked across a carpeted room, and he could see the books which rose from floor to ceiling along one wall. The late afternoon sun came in at a window where the blind wasn't drawn properly; apart from that, it was shadowy.

'Hallo, David,' she said.

Shawn didn't speak.

'How are you?'

Shawn still didn't speak, and the dislike Roger had felt for him came back, but he fought against it. Shawn was living in two different kinds of hell, he had never seen him except under dreadful pressure.

'I've brought Roger West,' Lissa announced. 'He's outside.'

'Should I care?' Shawn asked. His voice was still husky, but very tired, as if finding any words was a physical effort.

'He saw Ricky last night,' said Lissa.

Even without seeing Shawn's face, Roger sensed the tension which had clutched the man. A chair creaked. Roger moved forward, knowing that Shawn was coming towards the door. As he reached the doorway, Shawn was halfway from the window. Lissa stood against the window, and the shaft of sunlight caught her right hand and the side of her face. Shawn's face, against the light, looked dark and full of shadows, but his eyes burned. His hands were clenched by his side. He stopped moving, just stared.

Then, from across the landing, there came a scream.

20

SCREAMING BELLE

SHAWN moved convulsively, as if someone had stabbed a knife into his back. The scream came again, as a door burst open and a woman ran across the landing into the room. Now she was screaming all the time. Roger spun round. Belle Shawn was beating her hands against her breasts, her mouth was open as if it were locked that way. She wore a simple white dress buttoned down the front, the top button unfastened, and her fair hair was braided and drawn back from her forehead. In spite of the way her mouth stretched back, she still appeared beautiful – tall, full-breasted, with the figure of a Juno and the wildness of the demons in her eyes.

'Why don't you stay with me?' she screamed at Shawn. 'I

can't bear to be alone, you ought to stay with me. You don't care, that's the truth, you don't care about me. You don't care about Ricky. You're a devil, that's the truth of it, a cold, heartless devil. *Why don't you stay with me?*'

'But, Belle, you said —'

'I asked you not to leave me alone, I can't stand it! And all you care about is running after *her*. Why don't you go away with her? Why don't you? That would be better than tormenting me, torturing me!'

'Belle,' Shawn said, 'you asked me to leave you alone for an hour.'

'Answer my question! Why don't you go away with her? Do you think I don't know what's going on? In my own house, under my own nose. Think I don't know where you've been all the afternoon. In *her* bed, that's where you've been. You left me alone, just when I need you most. You went to her.'

'That's not true,' Shawn said in a dead voice. 'You know that's not true.'

'You can't fool *me*. I know. I've known for months. *I* could stay behind, but *she* had to come to England with you. You pretended it was work, all you wanted was to have that wanton with you. I won't have her in the house any longer. I won't have her!'

'You're not yourself,' Shawn said. 'Lissa's a good friend to us both. She—'

'Friend!' Belle screeched. 'She's your mistress, the whore, I won't have her in the house another minute.' She turned, looked as if she would fly at Lissa, beat at her, drive her out of the house by force. '*Get out, get out, get out!*'

Lissa stood without moving.

Shawn stretched out his long arm, and his fingers closed round his wife's wrist. She stopped, as if she knew that she had no hope of getting free.

'Be quiet,' Shawn said, and his voice became stronger. 'It's not true and you know it. Don't go on like this, Belle. I won't have it any more.'

'Send that whore away!'

'Belle, will you listen —'

She struck at him savagely, and he backed away and freed her wrist. She pushed again and he lost his footing and went staggering back.

Belle flung herself at Lissa.

Roger would rather have been a thousand miles away, but he couldn't just look on. The first time he had seen Belle Shawn, she had tried to push past him, and he had felled and stunned her. Now he thrust her to one side and stepped in front of Lissa, whose face was cold and set as an alabaster statue. Belle steadied, turned to fly at the new adversary, might have done so if Roger had not said:

'I saw your son last night, Mrs Shawn.'

Belle stopped absolutely still. Her arms fell by her side and at once the passion drained out of her cheeks and eyes. He had never seen anyone emptied of everything as she was then; he could not have stopped her more effectively if he had struck her. She stood quite still, legs a little apart, hands limp by her side. After a moment, the blankness of surprise faded from her eyes, but she didn't speak.

'Ricky's all right,' Roger went on quietly. 'I saw him and talked to him.' Nothing would make him tell the Shawns about the plaster over the boy's mouth. 'He told me they hadn't hurt him, and I could see that for myself.'

His back was turned on Shawn, his only concern then was Belle. Then a hand crashed on to his shoulder, fingers gripped him like claws. Shawn spun him round, and glared into his eyes.

His lips hardly moved.

'Don't lie!'

Roger said: 'To hell with you.' He doubled his right fist and drove it into Shawn's stomach, with all his weight behind it. The sudden surge of fury blinded him to what Shawn might do. Damn Shawn, damn this hysteria which made mockery of distress. Shawn staggered back, his eyes losing their fire as astonishment caught him, stumbling against a chair.

'I saw the boy, and he's all right,' Roger said harshly. 'If you had only behaved like a father instead of a mad bull, you might have had him back by now. Tell us what messages you get, help us find the kidnappers, instead of getting in our way.' Shawn, still dazed, gave no answer, and Roger turned on Belle. 'You're just as bad – in fact you're worse, you stop your husband from doing what he should. You're flagellating yourself with unnecessary horror. Lissa was driving with me all the afternoon. She's tried to help you both, and you've made it an ordeal for her. If she had any sense, she would leave you to manage for yourself.'

Lissa was watching him, and the corners of her lips were curved slightly. He didn't notice that.

'You – saw – *Ricky*,' Shawn said with slow disbelief.

'They took me, too. We were held at the same house. I got away. By the time I reached the police, Ricky had been moved, but the police are closer now than they've ever been. They'll find him, if you do what you ought to.'

Shawn said very simply: 'I would do anything in the world to find him. Anything in the world.'

Belle cried: 'You saw Ricky!' It was as if she had only now realized the truth. Roger half turned as she rushed at him and flung her arms round his shoulders, thrusting her face very close to his. 'You saw him, and – and he was all right. You swear he wasn't hurt. Swear it!'

'He wasn't hurt.'

'Swear it!'

'God help me, your son was not hurt, Mrs Shawn,' Roger said quietly. 'I spoke to him. I spoke to his kidnapper. I was told they didn't intend to hurt Ricky. They know that nothing is his fault, they've nothing against him.'

Belle dropped her arms; and the soft warmth of her moved away. She looked past him, at Shawn.

'David, did you – did you hear *that*?'

Shawn's voice was choky with emotion.

'I knew he was all right, Belle, I was sure they wouldn't hurt him.'

'Ricky's not hurt,' she said in a distant voice. 'He's all right, and – and this man's seen him. Oh, David.'

She didn't move towards him, her arms fluttered, then her hands went to her face, she buried her face in them and began to cry. Her shoulders heaved, but she stood still. Shawn went to her; he looked gigantic by her side. His arm went round her shoulders gently, and it was easy to think that he had forgotten Roger and Lissa.

Lissa took Roger's arm, and they moved away. On the landing they stopped, turned and looked back at the tableau; the strength of Shawn's arm seemed to have stilled the heaving shoulders.

Lissa took her hand away from Roger's, and they went downstairs together, out into the bright sunlight and then beneath the shade of trees between the house and the swimming-pool. Mosquitoes and flies hummed lazily. There were hammocks and a swing garden-seat. They sat down, Roger cautiously as pain twitched the muscles of his leg. He took out cigarettes which Sergeant Al had pressed on him.

'I wonder how long this new mood will last,' he said dryly.

'They need a shot of Roger West once every hour or so.' Lissa was still pale, as if the scene upstairs had really hurt her. 'Belle can be so very sweet. It's hard to believe, but she can. I wonder if this would have happened if David hadn't been forced to leave her so much.'

'How long have you known her?'

'Oh, for years. I've worked with David for ten. She's never

turned on me quite like that before,' Lissa added, and looked rueful. 'She sounded so convincing.'

'She chose the wrong afternoon.' He laughed, but it wasn't funny. 'When did she first show signs of strain?'

Lissa considered. 'A year ago, I suppose. She was always very temperamental, you would never have called her even-tempered. Nor David, for that matter.'

'And David has been a year on this special work that has to be done in England,' Roger said.

'Yes. Belle didn't want him to go. I remember the scene when he told her that he was leaving. She had tried hard to make him refuse the assignment. I think I was astonished when he decided he had to take it on. God knows he didn't want to. But he knew he was the most likely man to do the work. He hasn't had it easy, Roger, and he put first things first. You have to know David and what has happened before you blame him for anything.'

Roger waved away mosquitoes.

'Gissing could have started working on Belle a year ago, if it is an espionage job.'

Lissa said slowly: 'We always assumed that the trouble was because Belle missed David so much. Or at least didn't want him away from her. Nothing's ever suggested that Gissing started as soon as that.'

'Have you ever tried to talk to her about it?'

'No. These emotional outbursts didn't really begin until Ricky was taken away. That is, they didn't come into the open. We watched David closely, and there were accidents which might have been attempts on his life. Immediately we knew about the kidnapping, we saw the possibility that they were really planning to break David up, to bring him back here. And they have.'

The seat swung gently to and fro, and a soft breeze blew from the hills. It was very quiet and deceptively peaceful.

'They,' echoed Roger flatly. 'Gissing and who?'

Lissa didn't answer.

Roger stood up slowly, moved to a tree and leaned against the trunk, watching the wind play with Lissa's hair, watching the repose of her face, the grace of her body. He had no other picture in his mind.

'All right,' he said. 'When we find Gissing we might find who else is working with him. Or for whom he's working. It's time I got to work. Tony Marino said there might be a line on Gissing over here. Is there?'

'We thought so, but it didn't get us anywhere. We will find Gissing, and we will need you when we do, but not before. It might be hours, days or weeks. Take it easy for a spell, Roger. It's possible that things will be quieter here now, it's a pleasant place to stay. But if you prefer, you could go back to New York. It doesn't matter where you are, provided we can reach you quickly. I shall stay here unless Belle returns to that attack; if she does, then I shall tell Tony that I think I ought to leave. It will only make things worse for David.' She stopped, watching him closely, telling him that she was thinking of him as a man, not as a cypher in the search for Gissing; telling him everything he already knew, although no words had passed between them. 'Roger.'

'Yes?'

'What's in your mind?'

He stood away from the tree, and smiled. He considered, and then said deliberately:

'I hope I'm not away from home too long. My wife will find the time drags.' He watched her, and she made it clear that she knew exactly what he was saying, and would never try to make him wish that the words and the implications had not been made.

'Of course,' she said. 'I understand.'

She smiled.

Roger lit a cigarette and looked across the swimming-pool

to the hills beyond, the ranks of trees and the undulating parkland. A long way off a car was moving along a dirt road, and a cloud of dust rose up behind it.

'And I am also a detective,' he said huskily. 'That is how I earn my living. Remember?'

'I remember.'

'Someone drugged David and Belle before the boy was kidnapped. Remember that, too? Who did it was never discovered. The drug might have been in cigarettes, in coffee, in anything they ate or drank. The last report I saw showed no traces of any drug in anything at the house in Wavertree Road, yet the cups and saucers were dirty, it looked as if everything had been left as the Shawns left it. It was a smart job. The dope was a barbiturate, almost certainly. It takes quick effect. They didn't have it in the middle of the day, but quite late in the evening – say an hour or less, before they folded up. Ricky had been doped, earlier, probably with a smaller dose. Bill Sloan's very good. His report said that as far as he could find out – he talked to you about it, I think – the only thing that the child and the parents all ate or drank was the milk. It might not have been in the milk, but that's as likely as anything else.'

'Yes,' said Lissa. She was still relaxed; but her expression had changed, she looked at him intently, almost warily.

'Who could have doped the milk?' asked Roger. 'We haven't found that they had any visitors after you went. None of the neighbours noticed anyone. That's not conclusive, but it is a reasonable indication. There was no talk of visitors coming after you'd left. Was there?'

She shook her head.

'Remember I'm a detective,' Roger said quietly.

'Yes,' she said, without smiling. 'And the detective thinks I could have put the drug into the milk.'

'He knows you could,' said Roger, very slowly. 'He doesn't know whether you did. If he believed you did, he wouldn't know your motive. His chief trouble is that he can't be sure who else had the opportunity. Can you give him any help?'

21

URGENT CALL

LISSA put her foot against the grass and pushed gently; the seat swung to and fro. The quiet lingered about them, and there was no sound from the house. The hiss of water spraying from a jet merged with the sound of mosquitoes and flies. For a few moments Roger's mind was at peace, too. This fear had tormented him for hours, it was a relief that it was in the open. He had told her that there could be nothing between them more than the swift, unchallenged oneness which could never become a bond. She had accepted that. He thought that she knew what else was in his mind: a desperate desire to warn, to protect her.

'No,' she said quietly. 'I can't help, Roger.'

'Finding out could become a must.'

'Do you think Marino also wonders?'

'I don't see how he could fail to.' Roger moved, and sat beside her, and the swing moved suddenly and she was flung against him. He said fiercely:

'Don't make any mistake, Lissa. You're a natural suspect. There's overwhelming evidence that there is a leakage at the Embassy, too – the other side doped me within an hour or two of reaching New York, so there must have been a leak. Marino's not blind. Did you know when I was coming, and where I was to stay?'

She nodded, mutely.

Roger said abruptly: 'Were you here when Ricky was given his gold identity tag, to hang round his neck?'

She nodded, but looked puzzled.

'He dropped it by the side of the swimming-pool,' she said. 'It was dented at one corner – not much, but he was so upset he burst out crying. Belle cheered him up, I remember – she said there could never be another one just like it, no one would ever have a tag with a corner with that particular dent.'

'Who else was here?'

She was looking at him, head turned uncomfortably; their shoulders still touched.

'David had come home for a month's vacation. We were leaving next day for London – David and I. Carl Fischer was here, too. We'd all been in the pool, Ricky was learning to swim. The servants were about, of course.' Her eyes smiled for the first time since he had started these questions. 'Don't forget the servants, Roger.'

'Was any servant near the pool?'

'Ricky could have told his Nanny that he'd dropped the tag.'

'But none was near.'

'No.'

'David and Belle, you and Carl Fischer. Lissa, it's going to be important. This case is too big to take any chances. Was anyone else present that day?'

She turned her head and looked towards the swimming-pool, where the sun, now low in the sky, turned the blue water to gold. The lift of her head made a picture that was going to live in Roger's mind. She frowned a little, then looked round sharply.

'Yes. Ed Pullinger.'

'Are you sure?'

'Ed came late,' she asserted. 'He brought some letters for Tony and others of the Embassy. He didn't swim, but he was here when Ricky dropped the gold tag.'

'I certainly think our Ed wants watching,' Roger said, grimly. 'Ed Pullinger, Fischer and you, the three main suspects. Lissa, don't get any silly ideas into your head that you've got to protect anyone, or that you're safe from suspicion. If there is anything you remember that might point a finger at Ed or Carl, point it. *Stab* it. This thing can hurt you. It could ruin you.'

'You're a poor detective,' Lissa said. 'You should have kept all this to yourself.' She gripped his hand suddenly, and sprang up. 'Let's get to the house.' They walked slowly, side by side, and at the foot of the steps, she said: 'Thank you, Roger. But I didn't dope the milk.'

Her eyes were suddenly gay, and she ran up the steps ahead of him.

• • •

At dinner there was a brittle brightness. Belle and David Shawn both came down, Fischer was there, and Lissa and Roger. Now and again Belle would talk of Ricky as if she were now sure that it was only a matter of time before she had him back.

'It's wonderful to know he's not hurt,' she said a dozen times, always with the same forced brightness and with the flashing smile at Roger.

Shawn said little. The fire had dimmed in his eyes, and he looked as if he couldn't keep awake right through the meal. Fischer, after a sleep, was much fresher. All felt the strain of a wait which might end suddenly and might drag on for days. Would Belle last out in this mood, if it did? Roger watched her more closely than any of the others, but gave Fischer more attention than he seemed to. In England, he would have had plenty to dig into – Ed Pullinger especially. Lissa told him she had reported the reasons for wondering about both Ed and Fischer, but hadn't talked about it apart from that.

They were in the big lounge, after dinner, when Fischer said easily:

'I'm only the doctor around here, but I'd advise early bed

for everyone, the doctor included. David, you ought to get some sleep right away.'

'Could do with it,' Shawn conceded.

'Honey, let's have an early night,' Belle said, and squeezed his hand. 'I've kept you awake so much lately, if you get sick I'll just have to blame myself. You won't mind, will you?' she asked the others vaguely, and stood up.

It was a little after nine o'clock.

At ten, Roger looked out of his bedroom window over a starlit countryside, with the murmurs of the night for company. He was restless and uneasy, and knew that he wouldn't get to sleep if he went to bed. The peacefulness was unreal, even uncanny. Last night he had been on the way to Webster's house, beginning the ordeal that ended at the lakeside, now it seemed as if danger were a million miles away; and yet it might be lurking at every corner, every window. He had another gun which Fischer had given to him. He slipped it into his pocket, already accustomed to carrying one, and not finding it strange. He went out of the room, and walked through the silent house to the front door. The servants had gone to bed early; they slept in another wing. He opened the door, which was locked but not chained or bolted, and stepped on to the verandah.

He walked down the steps, slowly. He couldn't go far, if there were watchers the open door was an invitation; he must keep it in sight. It was cool; not cold, not even chilly, almost an English summer evening. The grass was firm underfoot. The hiss of the spraying water was silenced. He walked to and fro, seeing the shadowy darkness of the trees, much more clearly defined than on the previous night.

He saw no one, and heard nothing.

He stayed out for half an hour, then returned to the house, redropped the catch of the front door, and went upstairs. A sliding door on the landing led into his bedroom, which was large, airy and modern; inside the room, another door led to a small bathroom. He had as hot a bath as possible, to ease the tightened muscles in his legs and back, then put on borrowed pyjamas and went to bed. He was pleasantly tired now; the disquiet had been steamed out of him. It had been at least as much due to uncertainty about Lissa as to the thought of lurking danger.

He went to sleep.

Sound pierced his sleep vaguely – sound which might have been part of a dream. It woke him. He lay between sleeping and waking, and then heard the sound again. He turned his head slowly, and looked at the window, which was outlined against a greying sky; dawn. No one was there. He turned his head again, cautiously, and looked towards the door.

It was opening.

He loosened the bedclothes, and shifted his legs; a twinge of pain shot through his calf. He eased himself to one side, so that he could spring out of bed quickly, and watched the door through his lashes. For a moment he thought that the half-light had deceived him, that the opening of the door had been in his imagination.

It creaked.

Roger waited. Lying still and tense beneath the bedclothes, he flexed his muscles in readiness for the bound which was to bring him face to face with this unknown visitor.

Gradually, the door opened; and in the greyness of the morning a woman appeared. He could see her hair, the silhouette of her robe against a light beyond.

It was Lissa.

She stood for a moment looking at him, and he breathed evenly; she was listening for that. Then she came forward, without closing the door. Her right hand was stretched out, and he tried to see whether she had anything in it, but could not. She drew nearer, and her robe rustled, but otherwise she made no sound. Now she was only a foot or two from the bed, and he could see that her hand was empty. The light was good enough to show the softness of her beauty; and the robe seemed like a silken sheath. His heart was thumping with a fierce longing which he wouldn't face. She leaned forward, as if to make sure that he was asleep, and then, quickly, she bent towards him. He moved convulsively. Her lips touched his, pressed hard against them, and he became still.

She drew back, breathing heavily, more agitated than he had ever known her. Then she said softly:

'Roger.'

He grunted, as if he had been asleep and the movement had been unconscious.

'Roger,' she said more loudly. 'Wake up.' Her hand moved to the bedside lamp, and she switched it on. The brightness lit against his eyes, and he screwed them up. 'I'm sorry, Roger, but you must wake up.'

'Who's that?' he muttered.

'It's Lissa.'

'Lissa? What —' He didn't try to finish, but struggled up on his pillows. 'What is it?'

'There's been a message,' she said quietly. 'Marino thinks he knows where Gissing and Ricky are. You're to fly down to Trenton, New Jersey. I hated waking you.' She had easily won the brief fight against her emotional agitation. 'You sleep like a child.'

He said gruffly: 'But I'm not a child. Give me ten minutes.'

'I'll have some coffee ready,' Lissa promised.

'Fine.' He smiled, rasped a hand over his stubble, waited until she had closed the door, and then pressed his fingers against his lips.

'You bloody fool,' he said savagely. 'You damned fool.' He made himself picture Janet, at the house, as she had been when Lissa's cable arrived. 'You *bloody* fool!' he muttered, and began to fling on his clothes. He pushed borrowed shaving-gear and oddments into a borrowed bag, and was ready when Lissa tapped at the door. 'Come in.'

She carried a tray. She hadn't dressed, looked as bright and fresh as he had always known her, but was crisp and businesslike. There were rolls and butter, jelly and marmalade, as well as coffee.

'No one else is awake,' she said. 'I'll be back in five minutes, and I'll drive you to the airfield. The plane's waiting.' She went out without looking at him.

In six or seven minutes she was back, wearing the same beige shirt and wine red skirt as yesterday, with a short-waisted lumber-jacket type coat slung over her shoulders. She drank the cup of coffee he poured for her, and they hurried downstairs. They were at the front door, when a man called out sharply:

'Who's that?'

Lissa cried: 'Be quiet!'

It was Fischer, still in his dressing-gown, hair tousled, eyes bleary in the landing light. He was already halfway down the stairs.

'What the hell's all this?'

'Roger's been recalled,' Lissa said.

'*Recalled.*'

'It's the very devil,' Roger said. His cue was ready made, because Lissa was determined Fischer shouldn't be sure of the truth. And couldn't Fischer have doped that milk, as easily as Lissa? 'See you one day.' He waved, and opened the door.

Fischer was muttering something, and still coming down. He was at the open door when they drove out from the garage. He waved.

'Can our man be Carl?' Lissa asked.

'It can be anyone, male or female.'

She laughed, but did not sound carefree. She drove much faster than she had the previous day, and the waking countryside slipped by. They passed through a township with the needle at sixty. The airfield was on the far side, and he heard the engines of a 'plane warming up. It was a twin-engined machine with sleek lines. The pilot and one other member of the crew were waiting.

Roger turned to Lissa. 'Be careful,' he said. 'You —'

'I'm coming with you,' she interrupted. 'I've a grip with some clothes in the boot. I had to fool Carl.'

. . .

Greeting the pilot and his second-in-command, climbing into the aircraft behind Lissa, looking out of the window at the green fields, the stretch of tarmac and the small aerodrome buildings all seemed to crowd in on Roger. He had hardly sat down before they started to move. There were twenty-two seats, but they were the only passengers.

He sensed the smoothness of the 'plane as it was airborne. It circled once, and he saw the building again. Lissa was by his side, leaning back relaxed.

But as the machine climbed, and Roger also relaxed back in his seat, a darting thought drove relaxation away.

He knew that Lissa could have doped the Shawns; knew too that she could have betrayed him, Roger, before, although he didn't think so, hated to think so. Could she have hired this plane and hired the pilot?

22

THE WHEELCHAIR

'WE'RE nearly there,' Lissa said. 'There's Trenton.' She pointed to a huddle of houses thousands of feet below, a township set amid green countryside, rolling and pleasant. Even up here, they could see the winding ribbons of roads and, not far away, a road wider and straighter than the others. 'I wonder if they're right, and they've found Gissing.'

'We'll see,' said Roger, and forced out the question which he had locked in for the past hour and a half. 'Why did *you come the way you did*?'

'I knew Carl was up, there was a light under his door when I left your room. I thought if he saw me about in a robe, he would assume that I wasn't leaving. But naturally he had to see me fully dressed. If he's involved, he will have found a way of warning Gissing. I suppose I could, too.'

Roger shrugged. 'Everyone but Ed Pullinger. It might have been better to stay behind. Carl wouldn't have been suspicious of me leaving on my own.'

'I had to come,' Lissa said.

'Orders?'

Her eyes laughed at him. 'Yes, and not mine.'

They were circling to land, and Roger could pick out the small airfield and the little ant-like figures of men waiting for them. He still didn't feel sure of anything, but was less uneasy than he had been. The landing came, as always, before he expected it. They taxied towards the airport buildings, past them slowly once, and then turned back again. He felt Lissa become tense. They turned again and taxied back, and Lissa said softly:

'There he is.'

'Who?'

Roger peered out of the little window, and needed no answer. A man sat in a wheelchair outside the doors of the building. He wasn't smiling. He had a big face, and even from here his chin and jowl seemed dark. He was hatless, and his hair looked black as soot.

Marino had come home.

• • •

Marino's hand-clasp had the warmth of old, tried friendship. He smiled at Roger, then put both hands out to Lissa, who bent down and kissed him on the forehead. He chuckled as he began to turn the wheels of his chair. Roger and Lissa walked, one on either side of him, across the grass towards the cars which were waiting on the road leading to the town.

'I need more of that treatment,' Marino said. 'Have you two made it up?'

'Who's quarrelled?' asked Roger.

Marino's manner had a touch of boyishness which was good to see, which hid excitement and expectation; he seemed more than ever sure of himself.

'Didn't she quarrel with you, Detective?'

Roger looked over his head at a demure Lissa.

'Lissa reported it to Washington, I picked up a message,' went on Marino. 'It wasn't a laugh, either, Lissa had been pointed out as a suspect by others, but we always come down on her side. Carl Fischer – it would surprise me if he were anti-American, but I've been surprised before. Ed Pullinger? He was at the swimming-pool when Ricky dropped that identity tag. We can work on that later. Sure you'll recognize Gissing again, Roger?'

Roger said: 'If I had to forget you or Gissing, I would forget you. Where is he?'

'We think he's at a farm fifteen miles from here,' replied Marino. 'He answers your description. He was seen in a car early last night. There were two cars, the same make as two of the cars which left Webster's old house, and in the first there was a boy passenger, who seemed to be asleep. A traffic cop noticed them. He was directing traffic past an accident, they had to slow down, and he had a good look. So we checked. Several other people noticed the two cars, and three described Gissing well enough to make us hope. So we got into the garage during the night and scraped some of the dirt from under the guards. It's Adirondacks dirt, of a kind you don't find in New Jersey. There was a copy of the *Wycoma Standard* in the glove compartment, too, so the cars came from that neck of the wood. A man who could be Gissing, a sleeping boy and this evidence isn't conclusive, but why shouldn't we hope?'

'Don't ask me,' Lissa said. 'Why did you come yourself, Tony?'

'I was recalled. I have to talk David into going back to England.'

No one spoke.

Marino was helped into a big pre-war Lincoln, next to the driver, with Roger and Lissa at the back.

'We're going to a restaurant two miles away from the farm,' Marino said, 'and from there we're going to raid the house. It will catch them with their pants down. The farm's surrounded, and anyone who leaves is picked up when he's too far away to be noticed by anybody still at the farmhouse. It can't go wrong.'

He meant: 'It mustn't go wrong.'

'And when you've caught Gissing and found the boy, I just put a finger on Gissing,' Roger said.

'That's right.'

'Don't you like the plan?' Lissa picked out the doubt in his voice.

'I don't like it at all,' Roger said bluntly.

'How would you do it?' Marino asked, turning his head with difficulty.

'I could identify him first, you could catch him afterwards.'

'You would go up to the house on your own?'

'And have a better opportunity to get in. If he has time, he might kill that boy.' Roger's tone was light, but neither of the others needed telling what he was thinking. 'Let's give the boy a chance.'

'How would he think you'd found him on your own?' Marino asked dryly. 'We'll do it our way.'

'It's the wrong way.'

Marino sighed. 'These stubborn Britishers.'

'Oh, I know, I've been wrong all along,' Roger said heavily. 'If Fischer's the spy, Gissing will know that I'm on the way somewhere. Lissa tried hard, but Fischer wouldn't so easily be convinced that I was recalled to London. Even if Fischer didn't, someone else might have warned Gissing, and the chances are he will be ready for you when you arrive. You know all this as well as I do.'

'If Gissing's had a warning, he would be ready for us and ready for you. And if you went alone, he would know we weren't far behind,' Marino argued.

'Are we getting any place?' asked Lissa.

'We will do it my way,' said Marino. 'Sorry, Roger, but that's how it is.'

They drove on, the chauffeur apparently oblivious. Roger sat at the back, staring at Marino's head, knowing nothing would move the man yet feeling sure that to raid the house as Marino planned offered risks that could be avoided. The truth was simple: Marino was sure that he had Gissing surrounded, thought that when Gissing knew the game was up, he would submit without a fight. He didn't know Gissing.

Roger wished constraint had not fallen on all of them – a form of reaction because the end seemed to be near. Lissa didn't look at him. He studied her lips, and remembered . . .

He turned his head, and then heard a car horn blare out. It blared again, loud and shrill with warning. The driver swerved to one side, and a car flashed by, pulled in front of them and began to slow down. A man in the front passenger seat waved wildly. The driver put on his brakes, and looked at Marino.

'What'll I do?'

'It's Pullinger!' Lissa said. 'Pullinger's waving.'

'Okay,' Marino said to the driver.

'How much does he know?' Roger asked. The uneasiness

he had felt at Webster's house when Pullinger had been brought in, and which he had felt again at Wycoma, had never been stronger. 'About the farmhouse, I mean.'

'Nothing,' said Marino. He was frowning at Pullinger, who had climbed out of the car ahead and was running towards them. 'We didn't tell him. He didn't do a very good job with you in New York, Roger, but we haven't checked his story yet. I thought he was in Wycoma, he was told to stay there and go through the Webster house, pulling it apart.' He wound down his window as Pullinger came up, breathing heavily. His eyes glittered, as if he couldn't fight down excitement. 'Hi, Ed,' said Marino smoothly. 'How come?'

'Tony, have I got news for you!' Pullinger paused, as if for breath. 'I found plenty at Webster's house. The address of the farm.' He jerked his head backwards, and paused again. 'I called the office, and they told me you had an address already.'

'So what's news, Ed?'

'This is news,' said Pullinger. He pulled a gun from his pocket, and his grin was from ear to ear. 'Big news. Ready for more. I told the office you'd got the wrong farm. I had the cordon moved, no one is round Gissing's place now. How do you like the news, Tony?' He was still grinning.

The driver of Pullinger's car was standing at the other side of the Lincoln. His back was to passing traffic, but Roger could see his gun.

'You want to drive on, and have a talk with Gissing?' Pullinger invited.

. . .

Tony Marino didn't answer. Lissa leaned back, with her eyes closed; Roger had never seen her look tired before. In the bright morning two cars passed, drivers and passengers looking curiously at the old Lincoln and the Chevrolet in front of it. A big truck and trailer ground its way towards them, and Pullinger's man pressed closer to the car, to make sure there was room.

This answered many questions, but Pullinger had not doped the milk, had never been in England.

'You don't have to drive on,' Pullinger said. He looked absurdly young. 'But if you're not at the farmhouse in twenty minutes, the Shawns won't have a son named Ricky. Just imagine what that will do to David Shawn. Guess how much use he would be to you after that, Tony. Gissing might make a visit worth your while. Why not come along? Lissa and my old pal Roger can get into the Chevy, I'll keep you company. You want to get out, Lissa?'

He opened the rear door with his free hand. He didn't look evil, as Gissing could look, but just a fresh-faced, eager boy. He was taking a desperate chance. Traffic wasn't thick here, but there was traffic.

'I've grown to like Ricky,' he said. 'No one can blame the kid, can they? And you can't do anything to help now, Tony, unless you talk to Gissing. Why not try it?' Behind his airy brightness the strain was beginning to show. 'I said twenty minutes, and Gissing gets impatient.'

Roger couldn't see the expression in Marino's eyes, but he could imagine it. Lissa had opened her eyes, and her hands were clenched in her lap. Roger moved slightly, his side pressing against her leg; she must feel the gun which he had in the pocket, which she could get more easily than he. If there was a chance, it was now. Marino was holding Pullinger's gaze, Pullinger showing greater signs of strain.

Lissa noticed nothing, or preferred to pretend that she didn't.

'So you're on the other side, Ed,' Marino said softly. 'You're a traitor. I didn't think it could happen to you.'

Pullinger laughed, and the sound wasn't free.

'You can guess,' he said. 'You can guess wrong, too. It's time Lissa and my old pal from Scotland Yard got moving. And you're an important guy, Tony, I don't want anything to happen to you either.' He gave the laugh again. 'Get moving.'

'Do what he says,' Marino said slowly.

Pullinger exclaimed: 'That's my boy! Take it easy, Lissa. Don't try to pull anything, West.'

'Don't try to pull anything,' Marino confirmed. 'We'll see what Gissing has to say.'

'That's one thing about Tony Marino, he's full of good sound sense.' Pullinger was exultant as yet another car was waved past by his companion, who was still standing on the Lincoln's off side. He held the rear door wide open, and Lissa got out, Roger followed, his gun knocking against his side, twice. It didn't have a chance to do that a third time, for Pullinger slipped his hand into Roger's pocket and took it; he dropped it into his own pocket, and laughed again; his laugh was shrill. 'Get going, old pal,' he said.

Roger walked stiffly towards the Chevrolet, his arm brushing against Lissa's. She stared straight ahead of her, and seemed to be moving like clockwork. The man from the other side of the Lincoln walked behind them, a hand in his pocket, his gun hidden. Pullinger was already in the Lincoln, covering Marino and the driver.

Lissa said softly: 'Roger.'

He glanced at her. She didn't raise her voice.

'Roger, I don't think we'll see Gissing. We might talk to him, but we won't see him. You're the one on the spot. We might get away, but you won't.'

'Quit talking,' said the man behind them.

'Tell me a thing I can do,' Roger said.

She didn't answer. He didn't need an answer. He could try to tackle the man behind him, and might manage to get away. The road was empty but for the two cars, now; another might come into sight at any moment, but would it do more than bring others into the tragedy? This was complete and utter failure.

They were almost alongside the Chevrolet.

'I'm going to run,' Lissa said in that faint whisper. 'And you're going to run, when I've drawn fire. One of us will have a chance. Be ready.'

'Don't do it!' The man behind might hear his voice or at least the urgency of Roger's manner. He gripped Lissa's arm. 'Don't do it.'

'I'm going to run,' Lissa said. 'You'll have a chance that way.'

On the last word, she pushed him aside, then raced alongside the Chevrolet. Roger staggered against the side of the car. There was a wire fence along the road here, and beyond it an orchard of young fruit trees, but Lissa hadn't a chance to reach cover. Roger was still off his balance when he heard the shot and saw her fall.

23

THE FACE OF MARINO

LISSA fell headlong as the echo of the shot died away. She was still moving with convulsive jerks of arms, legs and head when Roger turned on the man behind him, who had shot her. If the gun had been pointing at his own chest and murder been in that man's eyes, it would have made no difference. Roger saw that the man was still watching Lissa; he could see nothing in the car behind. Swiftly he flung himself forward and downwards, arms outstretched to grab the gunman's legs. The roar of a shot blasted his ears as his arms folded behind the man's knees and he heaved.

The man pitched backwards, his hat flew off, his head crashed against the road.

There might be danger left, but not from the fallen man.

He lay as still as death, the gun a few inches from a limp hand; as Roger stood up, blood started to flow sluggishly, collecting the pale dust of the road. Now the danger came from Pullinger and the Lincoln. Roger snatched the gun, his finger on the trigger as he looked up, prepared for the winged bullet of death. Pullinger, Marino and the driver were puppets leaping and prancing between him and Lissa; the burning image on his mind was of Lissa, falling.

It faded.

Marino had turned in his seat, and it was almost impossible for Marino to turn. His face was just a cheek, an ear and the tip of a nose. He had twisted himself round so that his left arm was over the back of his seat, fingers buried deep in Pullinger's neck. His right fist, clenched, smashed and kept smashing into Pullinger's face, and already that youthful face was a scarlet running wound. There were other sounds, of car engines and car horns, but all that Roger really heard was the sickening thudding of fist against face.

The driver was plucking helplessly at Marino's wrists.

Roger made himself look round. A car had stopped, and two men were running towards Lissa, another car was drawing up alongside him, the driver shouting questions which he didn't hear. He could leave Lissa to others; he must. He ran to the door of the Lincoln, pulled it open, and struck Marino on the side of the head, a blow that would have knocked most men sideways. Marino kept smashing into the red mess. Roger struck him again, savagely, and Marino's grip on Pullinger's neck relaxed. The driver put both hands against Pullinger's shoulders and pushed; Pullinger fell back on the seat. Roger saw the driver lean over to take Pullinger's gun from the floor.

Marino moved round clumsily. Roger looked into a face so suffused with hatred that he himself could neither move nor speak. He didn't know how long he stood there. He was vaguely aware that motorists were approaching, warily because of the guns in his hand and in the driver's; and he saw, as if it were happening a long way off and had nothing to do with him, that the motorists stopped dead when they saw Marino.

At last Marino's gaze shifted, and he looked past Roger towards the orchard and the men who bent over Lissa. Roger didn't know that they were lifting her. He saw the transformation; it was like watching a devil turn into a saint. All hatred died. Yearning showed in Marino's eyes, and his face was touched with a softness that matched a mother's for a child; a lover's for his love.

He didn't speak or need to speak. Roger knew why he had succumbed to the red surge of rage, why he had changed now.

· · ·

A man said: 'Put that gun down, will you?'

'Don't get too near, Hank,' another warned.

'You heard me – put that gun down.'

Roger forced himself to look away from Marino and saw the motorists, two of them, Hank probably the nearer, a stripling wearing a peaked skull cap and a red lumber-jacket, whose long jaw was thrust forward and who was edging closer.

Roger swallowed.

'Has anyone called the police?' he asked. His voice was husky, but the words seemed to carry reassurance. He dropped the gun into his pocket, put a hand on Marino's shoulder and said: 'I'll look after her.' He hurried away, ignoring protests from Hank and his cautious friend.

Lissa was lying on her back, with a folded coat beneath her head, hair bared to the bright sun, body limp but eyes wide open. One of the men with her straightened up and hurried towards the road, glancing at Roger without stopping. But he called:

'Must get a doctor, quick.'

The other man was speaking to Lissa.

'Just stay where you are, you'll be okay. But don't move, honey, don't move.'

Lissa didn't move.

She was looking towards Roger, recognized him, smiled as he drew near. She looked pale, but didn't seem to be in pain. Blood stained her beige shirt-blouse, near the waist, and seemed to be spreading, and the men by her side stared down helplessly. If the blood came from one side it didn't matter, if it sprang from a wound in the middle of her body, it might be deadly.

'I'm all right, Roger,' she said. 'See, I'm learning the correct thing to say.'

'Now you keep quiet.' He smiled at her as he might at Janet, brusquely affectionate. 'Tony nearly pushed Pullinger's nose to the back of his head.' He stripped off his coat, knelt down and laid it on the ground, then gently tucked one side beneath her. The back of his hand came away red from the patch of blood. 'Does it hurt much?'

'It hardly hurts at all. It's beginning to ache a little.'

He unzipped her skirt at the side near the wound, his movements quick yet gentle. She wore a pair of white nylon panties and a narrow suspender belt; skin and belt were soaked with blood, and he still couldn't tell where the wound was.

'It fastens on the other side,' Lissa said.

'You'll have to buy yourself a new belt.' Roger felt for his knife; of course, Gissing's men must have taken it. 'Have you a knife?' He held out his hand, and the man fumbled in his pockets and produced a big one, opened the blade and thrust the handle towards Roger. 'Thanks.' Roger cut the belt carefully, and it sagged away. Blood pumped out of the wound and ran over his hand. The man gasped in horror. Roger glanced up at Lissa's eyes, seeing the anxiety which lurked in their honey-coloured depths.

'It won't kill you,' he said, steadily, 'it's too far to one side.' But it could. He took a clean handkerchief from his pocket and swabbed the wound, until he could see the actual hole in the flesh. 'Handkerchief,' he snapped to the other man, who began to fumble helplessly in his pocket. Slipping off his jacket, Roger unbuttoned his shirt, took it off, flung it at the man and said: 'Tear it, fold it into a wad.' He pressed his fingers against Lissa's flesh, found the bone nearest the artery, pressed tightly. He had to staunch the flow, or she would bleed to death.

'A doctor, too,' Lissa mocked.

'You don't need a doctor,' he said. 'You need a keeper. Lissa, one day I will – we all will tell you what we think about you. Just now, relax.'

The man gave him a wadded piece of shirt, but he didn't use it at once. The bleeding had stopped, but would start again as soon as he released the pressure.

The wail of a siren came clearly through the air.

'Police or an ambulance,' Roger said to Lissa. 'The ambulance will be here any minute, anyhow. You're going to have a long rest, but you'll be fine. There won't be a scar where it matters.' The sun was warm on his arms and back, his fingers began to ache. 'If you'd seen Tony,' he went on, 'you would have thought his world had come to an end. When he thought you —'

The wailing was much nearer now, a mournful herald of rescue or of doom.

Lissa said: 'I know just how Tony feels. Is he hurt?'

'If anyone's hurt him,' said Roger, 'you have. Not that I blame you.'

She didn't answer.

The wailing pierced his ears and stopped, and more wailing sounded from farther away. The first was a police siren, the second the ambulance. A young doctor took over quickly, and there was nothing more for Roger to do. The doctor grunted as if satisfied with what had been done so far.

Roger smiled down, and said easily:

'I'll see you soon, we'll get the other job finished now. Don't worry, Lissa.'

He turned away and walked quickly back to the Lincoln and the crowd around it. A traffic cop was talking to Marino, aggressively at first, then with a swift somersault into deference. Marino had conquered emotion, there was a pale copy of his smile for Roger – and a question shouting from his eyes.

'A month in hospital, I should think,' said Roger.

Marino drew in his breath, and relief glowed in his eyes.

'That's wonderful,' he said. 'Wonderful. Do you know how to get these folk away from here?' He waved to the pressing crowd, and cops started bellowing. Pullinger had already been taken out of the car and was lying, unconscious, by the roadside. He would probably never recognize his face again. 'Get in behind me,' Marino said. Roger obeyed, and the driver started the engine, one of the traffic cops clearing a path. They drove slowly through the crowd. Marino looked out of the window at Lissa and the doctor bending over her, the ambulance men waiting for instructions. He waved. Lissa's head was turned towards him, and she smiled. Marino dropped his hand, stared straight ahead for a minute, then drew a great breath and spoke in a clear voice. 'Listen, Roger. Pullinger wasn't as good as he thought, our men were suspicious. No one was drawn away from the farmhouse, but the house Pullinger named was cordoned off as well. Now we'll raid —'

'Not your way nor my way,' Roger said sharply. 'Stop, driver.' The man braked, and Marino half-turned his head, ready to lay down the law. 'I'm going up to that farmhouse with as many men as you like,' said Roger. 'We'll take Pullinger's car. Gissing will recognize it, and it will fool him. I can wear Pullinger's coat and hat, too.'

Marino ran thumb and fingers over his chin.

'Go and get that Chevy,' he said. 'My God, you British

are stubborn! I'll go on. We'll meet at the restaurant, a mile along the road.'

• • •

Pullinger had said that Gissing would wait twenty minutes, but that could have been bluff. It could have been in earnest, too. The tumult of the hold-up was stilled, but a new storm blew, and Roger's mind's-eye picture of Ricky Shawn's face hid everything else. The bright, frightened eyes and the plastered lips, the frail arms with the cruel steel bracelets round them, were all vivid. There was nothing Gissing would not do. It had been a mistake to say that he would take Marino's men in the car, he ought to go alone. Alone, he might be able to bargain; with others, Gissing would know that the end was inevitable and might kill for the sake of killing. These thoughts pressed sharp against Roger's mind as he stood outside the restaurant by the side of the Lincoln, with several clean-limbed men standing nearby, waiting for Marino's orders. Marino was talking to the man in charge.

Roger went to him.

'You all ready, Roger?'

Roger said: 'Whenever you like.' He hesitated, looking straight into Marino's eyes. Then he said very carefully: 'Tony, I know I've a wife and two sons waiting for me in England. I know the risks. I still want to go alone. Give me the chance. In half an hour you can come and get me.'

Did Marino know exactly what he meant? Did Marino know that he was saying that whatever Lissa felt about him, there was a call from England that he would never be able to resist? He wished he could guess what was passing through the maimed man's mind. Whatever it was took a long time.

Then Marino said abruptly: 'Half an hour. All right. But listen, Roger. In half an hour, a light bomber will fly over that farmhouse and drop a bomb in the garden. It will shake them so badly they won't have any fight left, and my men will be in the house before the echoes have died away. Do you understand?'

'Nice work,' Roger said.

'Tell him how to get there, Stan,' Marino said to his driver.

The directions were easy – he must continue along this road from Trenton for a mile and a quarter, then take the first turning to the left on to a dirt road which dropped down towards a creek, swinging left again before the creek, uphill, with bush on either side, then down again to the farmhouse and the outbuildings. Roger followed the route carefully, and soon the Chevrolet was swaying along the rough road towards the rippling stream. At the brow of a hill he looked down over the farm, a big white weatherboard building, emerging from fruit trees and bushes.

Nothing, no one moved.

Approaching the house, he passed a cow-byre. Beyond it, pigs were rooting and Roger wrinkled his nose at the stench. A few hens scratched, one of them close to the front door, which had once been painted white but was now dirty, the paint peeling. Mud had splashed up in the rain, more than two feet from the ground. Roger sat in the car for a few seconds, to give anyone inside time to know that he was there and to make sure that he was alone. Then he got out and stood upright, looking round. He knew that eyes were turned towards him, that each window threatened, but nothing happened. He walked stiffly down two cement steps to the door, and banged on it.

Still nothing happened.

He clenched his fist and banged again, and when no one answered, he turned the handle and pushed the door. It opened. Would Gissing leave it unfastened? Would he let him walk in, like this? Were the watching eyes and the menacing demons all in his imagination? Was the house empty, and the Shawn child gone?

He stepped straight into a low-ceilinged room. The windows were small, and the light poor. The room was crowded with old furniture, and a spinning-wheel stood in one window with a chair drawn up beside it, as if some old woman had been working there only a few minutes ago.

Doors led to the right and left. He went towards that on the left, with his hands in sight, and his face clear of expression, all his fears held on a tight leash. He was prepared for anything – even for the voice which came from behind him.

'Don't move,' a man said.

24

TERMS

ROGER did not move.

He heard footsteps behind him, and he steeled himself for whatever would come next. For a moment he heard heavy breathing, as hands touched his sides and ran over his body, feeling for guns in pockets or in a shoulder-holster. He carried none. The breathing was hot on the back of his neck, and then coolness followed as the man backed away.

'Okay, just move forward, up them two steps.'

These steps led into a dining-room, a room almost as crowded with furniture as the first. He had been here for five minutes, and Marino wouldn't give him a second beyond his half hour.

'Turn right, and up the stairs,' the unseen man ordered. It sounded like McMahon.

The stairs led off a small hall, a flight of narrow, steep steps covered with carpet. He steadied himself by the handrail. The stairs creaked, and one tread sagged badly.

'Room on the right.'

He turned right.

He shouldn't have been surprised, but he was. Ricky lay on a bed in a corner of a narrow room, exactly as he had been at Webster's house – only more frightened, much more frightened. But at least he was alive.

Roger paused, steadied, then went into the room. He forced himself to smile without strain, raised a hand to the boy, and spoke in a voice that surprised him by its calmness.

'Hallo, Ricky. Glad to see you again.'

The child lay staring, without moving a muscle, but his eyes, his father's eyes, seemed to burn as savagely as his father's, with an animal fear.

'We'll soon have you free,' Roger said.

'That's right,' Gissing said. 'You will.'

He was behind Roger, but the voice was unmistakable, he was here in person.

'You will soon have him free,' Gissing said. 'It will cost you something, that's all. It will cost Uncle Sam half a million dollars. It's cheap at the price. They'll have the kid's father back as well as the kid. Half a million dollars, West, I'll settle for that. Turn round.'

• • •

Roger turned slowly.

Half a million dollars. It was only a set of figures, and it meant just one thing: that Gissing was prepared to come to terms. There was a chance to fight for Ricky's life.

Gissing stood in the doorway. Jaybird leaned against the wall, his mouth working as he chewed, a gun held casually in his big right hand. He seemed to look at Roger through his lashes.

Gissing wore exactly the same clothes and the same cotton gloves. A bruise on his right cheek showed red and swollen, even in the poor light. He held his head up, the narrow, pointed chin thrust forward, and he looked as full of confidence as he had been at Webster's house.

'You heard me,' he said.

'Only half a million,' Roger said dryly. 'You've had a hundred thousand from Shawn. Isn't that enough?'

'Half a million,' Gissing repeated, 'or I kill the kid and hang his body out of the window. I know Marino's got his men round the house, Pullinger didn't fool him. I know what happened on the road, I've had a telephone message. I know Marino has given you a chance to save the kid, and you think you're so smart that you can do it, but only one thing can do it, West. Half a million dollars.' He opened his thin mouth and laughed in the back of his throat. 'I'm holding up Uncle Sam now, Shawn hasn't got enough for me. Can't you see the joke?'

Roger didn't speak.

Gissing changed his tone. 'We won't waste time.' He looked past Roger to the child, could see the terrified eyes, and seemed to wring sadistic satisfaction out of repeating: 'If Marino doesn't persuade Uncle Sam to pay, I'll hang the kid out of the window, by the neck. Once that happens Marino can say goodbye to Shawn. It depends how badly he needs the man. Go and tell him, West. You can be useful that way. You ought to be dead!'

'Why did you leave me alive?'

'Jaybird thought I'd finished you off. I thought he had. But it was too late at Webster's place.' How clearly that betrayed the panic they had been in. Even now, Roger sweated at the hair's breadth between life and death. 'Tell Marino something else,' Gissing went on. 'If he moves his men in, he can write the kid and Shawn off. The only chance he's got is to withdraw the guard and come to terms. There isn't any other way.'

Roger said: 'And I'm to tell him that?'

'You can go back as free as you came, and tell him just that.' Gissing laughed at the back of his throat again. 'You came to find out the terms, didn't you, West? Now you know. Marino will play because he can't afford to lose Shawn. We needn't waste any more time.'

After a pause, Roger said slowly: 'I'll tell him, but he'll want more than Ricky. He'll want to know if you're working for anyone, he'll want to know how you got your information – how you learned I was coming here, how you knew about the gold identity tag. Was it Fischer?'

'After I've got the money I'll tell him everything he wants to know,' said Gissing. 'The full story of how one decadent Englishman held up the great Uncle Sam.' He laughed, and raised his hands. 'Don't waste any more time.'

Roger moved back, sat on the foot of the boy's bed and smiled up into Gissing's face. There was no window near the bed, and little danger, so Roger hoped, of broken glass hurting the child. As Roger had guessed, this move wasn't at all what Gissing expected, and his show of confidence began to wear thin. At heart, Roger knew, Gissing must realize that the odds were all against him, that his best hope was to get away alive.

'Decadent's right for you,' Roger said. 'And dumb. You haven't got even any commonsense left. You want Marino to play, but you ought to know that Marino's big worry is whether there's a power behind this kidnapping, a power which wants Shawn put out of action. Who's the money for? If it's for yourself, then he might play. I don't say he will, but he might. If you can convince him that it's just a ransom racket, it will take a big load off his mind, but if he thinks that there's a hostile power in the offing, he'll worry about breaking up this spy-ring first and worry about Shawn afterwards. Who are you working for, Gissing? Don't waste any time, because Marino gave *me* an hour.'

Would Gissing believe that?

Fifteen minutes had passed; at least fifteen.

Gissing said roughly: 'So he gave you a time limit.' He

tried to laugh, but it didn't come off. He looked at his wrist-watch swiftly, then moistened his lips with the tip of his tongue. 'I'll tell you the size of it,' he went on. 'No one's behind it except me. Just me. The kid was easy. We doped him, and when he came round on the way to the airport, he was helpless with tiredness. McMahon doped him again on the aircraft, he was half asleep when they got off at Gander. I knew Shawn would pay for him. Then I found out what Washington thought of Shawn. They can pay, too. I was over here on business when I discovered it. I had a spy in Shawn's household.'

'Who?'

Gissing moistened his lips again, then shrugged the question away. There was no reason why that should jolt Roger's mind into an idea which grew big, crowding a lot of other things out, but it did. It was an idea he'd had before but not so clearly.

'Who paid you that hundred thousand, Gissing?'

'You'd like to know. I'll tell you this: Ed Pullinger located me and sold me the idea of holding up Uncle Sam. I did the deal because a spy in the FBI would always be useful, but for this job I raised the ante.

'I had used Americans to work for me because I wanted Marino to believe that he was dealing with renegade Americans. In London, you caught on to the car and on to me quicker than I thought you would. Things took a bad turn. Ed cracked and had to go. But I had the boy, so I could make Shawn do what I wanted. That way I held all the aces, and I've still got them in my hand. There isn't any spy-ring. Ed Pullinger simply needed money, and *I'm* going to get plenty. I'm still sitting pretty.' He flashed his watch again. 'Go and tell Marino what will happen to that kid, West.'

There couldn't be more than five minutes to go, but even when believing there was thirty-five, Gissing was nervous.

'So you were that clever,' Roger said heavily. 'You

snatched the son of a man whom Washington would fight like hell for, which would bring out the FBI in force. Brilliant reasoning. Why bring Ricky here? Why take that chance in getting him out of England? Why did you want him in the United States so badly?'

Gissing said harshly: 'Haven't you got a mind? I wanted dollars. Shawn couldn't pay in dollars in England. I wanted to come over here, things were hotting up for me in Europe. There was a chance to get myself a dollar fortune. I didn't know how important Shawn was when I started, only that he was rich.'

The story could answer most things, but it left something out; the spy in the Shawn household – one who would help Gissing but hadn't told him how important Shawn was.

An aeroplane droned, not far away, and was drawing nearer.

Gissing snapped: 'That's all! Go and tell Marino about that half-million.'

He didn't expect to get it, of course, now he was just fighting for a chance to escape. He should have been satisfied with the money he'd got from Shawn, but greed had trapped him. He must have known he was finished but would not admit it.

The aeroplane seemed directly overhead.

There was another sound, of something coming down, a screeching, threatening whine which spanned the years, took Roger back to moments when he'd crouched or dived for cover. Gissing also knew the sound, and glanced upwards, mouth open. Jaybird looked puzzled. Roger braced himself.

The screech ended in a thunderous roar, the house shook, glass splintered and stabbed across the room, two pieces stuck into Gissing's face, a piece cut the tip of Jaybird's nose. That was the moment when Roger sprang. Getting the gun was like taking a toy from a child. He put a bullet through the gunman's knee and one into Gissing's chest, too high to kill.

Then all he had to do was shield Ricky's body and watch the door, gun in hand. He kept talking to the boy, trying desperately to calm the tormented mind, and was still trying when Marino's men came racing up the stairs.

• • •

Marino did not miss a thing.

Immediately after the raiding party came an ambulance with two nurses, and the child was taken by the nurses and whisked away, to the balm of sedation. Afterwards there could be peace for him and freedom from torment and reunion. Or there could be more distress.

The news about Lissa was good; she was no longer in danger.

Marino sat in the Lincoln, watching his men come out with their prisoners; three, as well as Gissing, Jaybird and McMahon. The bomb had landed twenty yards away from the house. One corner had been shattered by blast, and there wasn't a whole window left. A small fire had started from an oil-stove in the kitchen, but it was out already. The boy had gone, and Gissing was being carried on a stretcher towards a second ambulance. Marino looked away from the house towards the man, then up at Roger.

He'd heard the story; he didn't know about Roger's idea – his guess, his theory.

'And you believed Gissing,' he said, thoughtfully.

'It could be true,' Roger said. 'If Pullinger has a voice left, you can check with him. It would answer most things, wouldn't it? You don't *want* a spy angle, do you? You know where the leakage was in your department, and the only worry you have is about the leakage in the household, because that will matter to Shawn.'

Marino fingered his chin; his knuckles were bruised. Gissing was in the ambulance and the engine started.

'Meaning Carl Fischer? I've known Carl a long time.'

'You'd known Pullinger a long time,' argued Roger. 'Don't forget your big worry will be convincing David Shawn that it won't happen again.'

'We could convince David,' Marino said, 'but it won't be so easy with Belle.'

Roger looked at him levelly, and knew that they hadn't been thinking along parallel lines; if his guess were right, it would take Marino completely by surprise. Was it a guess? It was all circumstantial evidence, but he'd begun many a successful murder hunt on less. He could think more clearly now, but he hadn't much time.

'Do we have to stay here?' he asked.

'No, I'll come back and have a look later,' said Marino. 'We'll go into Trenton. I've had a man call David, he and Belle will be at Trenton as fast as an aeroplane can bring them. Get in, Roger.'

Roger got into the back of the car, and the driver, who seemed never to say a word, started off. Several men waved. A crowd had gathered near the creek, thirty or forty people whose ranks were swelling every minute. Marino seemed hardly to notice them, and did not speak until they were on the road and driving past the restaurant. Then he turned his head as far as he could turn it with comfort.

'You don't talk enough,' he said. 'I know how you feel about Lissa. I also know you for a man who won't make a fool of himself. You suspected Lissa once, in spite of the way you felt, but you can't suspect her now. We know there was someone besides Pullinger, we know it wasn't Lissa, so we shall have to have a talk with Carl Fischer, and I'm not going to like it. You agree?' He was almost aggressive.

'You could talk with someone else.'

'Who?'

'Someone who knew about that damaged corner of the gold identity tag. Someone who once had a fortune and lost it. Someone who could torment a man she was supposed to love, who stayed married to him because of his money, and whom money would have set free. Someone who did her devilish best to make her husband turn against her, because if he gave her freedom he'd give her money to make it real. But he wanted her too much. Someone who could fly into a rage and shout and scream and claw at her husband's face – and then calm down as if a tap had been turned off. Someone who could pick up that money and pass part of it on, keeping the rest for herself – to live on when she left her husband.'

Marino strained his neck to look round, opened his mouth as if to cry: 'No!' but didn't speak.

'The one woman who could influence Shawn enough to make him turn his back on working for you and all it meant,' Roger went on. 'Who was already making life hell for him, and would listen to anyone else who would help her get free. Someone she didn't love, but hated.'

Marino said hoarsely: 'No. Not the boy's mother.'

'Grant her that Gissing convinced her that Ricky would never be hurt, and what makes it impossible?' Roger asked.

25

REUNION

BELLE looked younger. She had freed her hair, and it hung down in waves to her shoulders. She wore a pale-green linen dress trimmed with yellow, carried a green handbag, and wore attractive green shoes. In spite of the dress and the air of simplicity, she seemed to offer a particular kind of sensual ripeness. She greeted Roger as if he were a friend who made her heart beat faster, yet she clung to Shawn's arm. He dwarfed her.

He looked like a man at rest.

They had come from the private room in the hospital, where Ricky lay sleeping. Marino and Roger were waiting at the hospital gates, Marino in and Roger by the side of the Lincoln. As Belle had walked towards them, Marino had said:

'If you're wrong, he'll kill you.'

'If I'm right, he'll always be on bail from hell,' Roger had answered.

'It's so wonderful,' Belle greeted them brightly. 'He looks so *peaceful*. And he hasn't been hurt, you were right, they didn't hurt him. His lips are red where that plaster was stuck on, but that will soon go, and the doctor says he'll be fine. Roger, how can David and I *ever* thank you?'

Shawn gulped. 'I wish I could even try.'

'We're staying until we can take him away, of course, it'll be two or three days. *Do* come and stay with us, Roger.' Belle put a hand on his, squeezed and wouldn't let go. 'He must, David, mustn't he?'

'He couldn't say no,' said Shawn.

Every minute that Shawn lived in this fool's paradise would make the revelation hurt more. They could wait in the hope that Gissing or Pullinger would talk, but Pullinger wouldn't be able to do so for twenty-four hours or more. In twenty-four hours Roger hoped to be flying home, to the good things there. If it would have helped he would have stayed here for weeks, but this had to be done with the swift incision of a surgeon's knife.

'One thing stops me staying here,' Roger said. The enormity of the accusation and the likely fury of Shawn's reaction swept over him, and he paused. Marino's eyes were on him. He put his hand into his pocket as if for cigarettes, and wished he had a gun. Shawn might be cataclysmic. 'Only one thing, Mrs Shawn. I've two sons of my own. They mean a great deal to me.' Her great eyes were fixed on his, and he thought that she had some inkling of what he was going to say; if he were right in that, then he was right about the rest.

'That makes it hard for me to sit at the same table, even to breathe the same air as you.'

She didn't speak.

Shawn seemed too stunned to resent the insult, if he understood it.

'Gissing didn't think I would ever get away alive,' Roger said. 'So he told me. How you hated your husband's job, worked on your husband's nerves – that was nothing new – and agreed to help with the kidnapping. Gissing gave you the drug, and you used it. You told him how the dent in the identity tag had been caused, and he pointed it out so as to prove he had Ricky. You knew him for a devil, and you made it easy for him to kidnap the child. You believed him when he said Ricky wouldn't be hurt. My God, how any woman could take a chance like that, any *mother* —'

'But he *wasn't* hurt, was he?' she cried. 'Gissing kept —'

She didn't add 'his word'. She spun round, and her gaze was on Shawn, who was staring at her while the truth seeped awfully into his mind. Roger had thought that Shawn would want to kill, but all he did was to keep looking at her, his features gradually stiffening, until he groaned as if in agony, and buried his face in his hands.

• • •

Hours afterwards, Gissing answered all their questions, soon there was nothing left that they did not know. Belle was under a form of house arrest at the hotel, Shawn was waiting in another room. He was not the caged tiger Roger had expected but a stony-faced man who spoke and acted mechanically, and whose eyes were like the embers of a dying fire.

Roger was glad that he would have no part in clearing things up, that the case was finished for him. Marino had not suggested that he should stay longer; it was as if the other man knew of his compelling reasons for wanting to get home.

Roger was alone in his room at the hotel when the telephone bell rang. It was early evening.

'Hallo.'

'Come down and see me, Roger, will you?' It was Marino, who had a room on the ground floor.

'Yes, right away.'

Marino, in the wheeled chair which couldn't be disguised, sat alone, smoking, a drink by his side. He waved to whisky and a soda siphon. He looked more settled in his mind, no longer as if he were trying to work out an insoluble problem. Almost casually, he said:

'I've just seen Lissa, she's come round. The bullet was lodged just beneath her ribs, but they've got it out.' He smiled almost drolly. 'There was talk about prompt action saving her from bleeding to death.'

'I couldn't be more glad,' Roger said warmly.

'I knew you would want to know. I've seen Shawn, as well. It's too early to be sure what will happen. I don't know what we'll do with Belle, or whether there will be a charge. I should think, no. She didn't know about the murder, simply made a deal with Gissing, whom she knew slightly. She raged about being tied to Shawn in Gissing's presence, and he told her how to get free. Fake a kidnapping, he said, and make Shawn pay up, then share the ransom. She probably passed on half of what Shawn paid, through Pullinger; we found it in her room. We could make a charge, you could make one in England, but I should still think no. Agree?'

'Provided she can't harm Ricky again.'

'There's no question of that. She and Shawn will part, of course – *will* part? They've parted. I think she had almost stifled his love for her, during the past few months he was clinging to it only because he thought it was the one way to keep Ricky. His folk will go to the Connecticut house and make it ready for the boy. He talks of making Belle an allowance, enough to live on. You never liked Shawn, did you?' Marino's lips puckered.

'We could use more Shawns,' said Roger.

'I won't even guess at the way it will work beyond that, Roger. Except that Shawn is going back to Europe. He'll have a month or so here, and then start work again. He might take Ricky with him.

'I've seen Gissing again,' Marino went on. 'I've talked to Pullinger, Jaybird and the others. It all adds up to the same thing – that Gissing didn't lie to you. It began in a small way, but when Gissing realized how high we rated Shawn, he thought he could make it much bigger. Pullinger located him and asked what silence would be worth – that's how they got together. Pullinger was always very clever. He had himself drugged at the same time as you, called another of our men, but didn't expect to get on to the car you were taken off in. When the other man came upon it, Pullinger played it out, leading the way as if by chance to Webster's old house. His colleague was kidnapped, he "escaped". It sounded fine.'

Marino paused.

'No Red scare case, after all. You've guessed, I suppose, that we were as nervous of a Red scare in the Press as we were of anything, there's trouble enough without that. If the Press had got hold of a Red angle – I needn't tell you.'

Roger laughed. 'I've been looking through some of your newspapers. I see what you mean.'

'It wouldn't do to have the whole of the world's Press as cold-blooded and austerity-ridden as yours,' said Marino slyly. 'Well, Roger, I guess that's about all, except just one thing. As soon as you can fix it, I want you and your wife, and the boys as well if you'll bring them, to come here for a vacation. A month, two months, as long as you like. You'll be our guests. Will you do that?'

'Even you wouldn't dare try to stop Janet if she hears of it,' Roger said softly.

'I'll write to her tonight,' promised Marino. He sipped his drink. 'Well, I guess that really is all.'

Roger finished his drink and poured himself another, sat back and stretched his legs out. 'How long will Lissa be in hospital?'

'Two or three weeks, they say, and then twice as long convalescing at home. Then she'll come back to work with me. Would you like to see her before you leave?'

'I don't think so,' said Roger. 'Just give her my love, and tell her I'm looking forward to seeing her in London. If she's interested, I'll take her round the Yard one day.'

• • •

He arrived at London Airport in the small hours, and as soon as he had passed through the Customs, there was Janet to meet him. There were fifty or more other people waiting with her, but he saw only Janet; and he saw her as if he were really looking at her clearly for the first time. She gasped when he hugged her, but the light in her eyes did him good. They didn't say much.

The Yard had sent a car and a driver, and they sat in the back and were driven through the dark streets of the suburbs and of London. The glare of the lights of New York seemed like a dream; and it wasn't the only thing that had been a dream.

There was nothing in it that he wanted to forget, now; just a little he didn't want to share with Janet; he could share everything else. The swift onslaught of unwanted passion had caught but never conquered him, and he had no regrets.

• • •

Marino's letter arrived and brought its sensation to Bell Street. They wouldn't be able to go for several months, but that didn't stop Janet from planning or the boys from talking. It was still the chief topic of discussion at the turn of the year, when Roger left Bell Street one morning, knowing that it would not be long before he would have to set a date so that they could start counting the days. He had a curious reluctance to telephone Marino. He knew that Lissa was back in England, and had twice had dinner with Shawn, who had brought Ricky with him in the charge of a middle-aged woman who had thawed most of the ice of fear out of the boy's mind.

At his office, the telephone rang.

'West speaking.'

'It's a Mr Marino, Mr West, from the United States Embassy.'

'Oh! Put him through.'

'Is that you, Roger?' Marino asked, and his voice was filled with warmth.

'Hi, Tony!'

'Hi yourself. When are you taking your family to see God's own country?'

'You're going to have a shock soon,' Roger said. 'I can't hold 'em back much longer.'

'Make it as soon as you can. Spring is a wonderful time in the Adirondacks! Don't keep putting it off, Roger. That invitation comes from Lissa, too.'

'Just give me time to soften my chief up.' He paused for Marino's chuckle. 'How is Lissa?'

'She's just fine,' said Marino, 'and she'd like to talk to you.' Marino paused, as if he knew that Roger might want a moment to get used to that; but he needn't have paused. 'Before she does, I've some news for you. About Lissa. She can't be sane, Roger, she surely can't be sane. She's going to marry me. How do you like that?'

Lissa's voice sounded in the background.

'He'd better like it. Let me talk to him.' A moment passed. 'Hi, Roger,' Lissa said. 'Tell Tony it's the sanest thing I've ever done, will you?'

'Sanest?' He stopped himself from saying 'bravest'. 'Luckiest!'

It was good to hear her laughter.